M. AINIHI

The Warning Signs

Tales Of Horror And Dark Fantasy

Ainihi, M. (2018) Cultivating Wrath. Ink and Sword: Issue 7 (Original work published in 2018)

First edition

ISBN: 978-1-7345618-3-8

Illustration by Tauseef Ahmed
Cover art by Rebecacover
Editing by Allister Thompson

This book was professionally typeset on Reedsy.
Find out more at reedsy.com

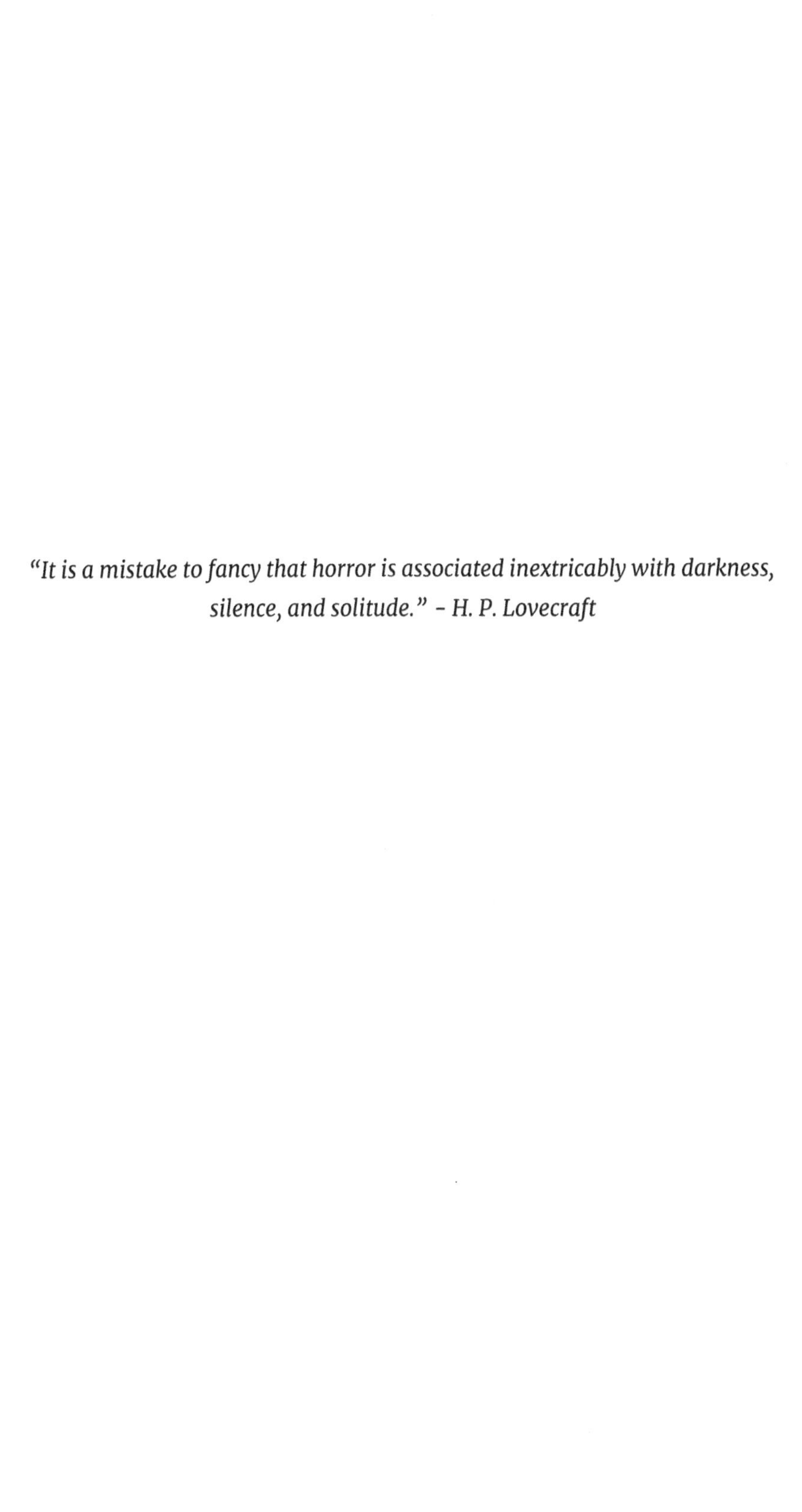

"It is a mistake to fancy that horror is associated inextricably with darkness, silence, and solitude." – H. P. Lovecraft

Contents

I

One-Shot Shorts

Perception

Joey had underestimated the utter blackness of nighttime in the forest. The silvery moonlight only trickled through the full branches of the densely packed trees that loomed high above, and he had to squint to see the dusty, rutted footpath he had planned to follow.

As he moved deeper into the woods, the aroma of rich earth and rotting leaves seemed heightened with the pressing darkness, as if his sense of smell was elevated by his lack of sight. The strong odor caused his stomach to twist and his throat to feel dry.

Joey traced the button on his heavy flashlight with his thumb for reassurance. He had installed new batteries just before he left his house. He had wanted to be sure that it would emit a strong beam that would cut through the darkness like a knife, but he didn't press it. To do so would be to admit defeat, and he couldn't. Not yet.

Samantha had followed him blindly into the woods, after all, and he didn't want to risk looking weak in her eyes. He concentrated on the sound of her footsteps behind him as he pressed on, trying to ignore the frantic beating of his own heart.

He shouldn't have let go of her hand. She hadn't seemed to mind when he took it at the path's edge, where the trail led into the darkness of the woods, but when the beads of sweat began to form on his forehead despite the cool air, he was worried that she would notice his increasingly sweaty palm against hers, and so he had released it.

"Joey, when will we get there?" Samantha whined. "My feet hurt from all this walking."

Confident that she was exaggerating, his cheeks warmed as her words settled in his ears. She had already made it a point to tell him that she wasn't supposed to be out in the woods tonight, more than once. So why had she given in so easily and joined him?

"Joey?" she asked again, raising the pitch of her voice even more. "No one ever comes out here and it's very dark. I'm scared."

"Shush, Samantha, we walk faster when you're quiet." His words came out harsher than he anticipated, and he regretted the statement almost immediately. After months of living here, she was still the only person he would consider a friend.

When he had first noticed that none of the other students talked to her either, he had mistaken her quietness for shyness and assumed that she was new to town as well. He had since learned otherwise, and he found her situation rather perplexing.

With her slender frame, fair complexion, and wavy chestnut hair, Samantha was what he considered a real beauty. He was certain that young men at his old school would have been fawning over her at every opportunity. As the days turned into weeks, he marveled at the way not only his fellow students, but also even his teacher seemed to give her a wide berth when she came near.

Although Samantha did confirm to him that she had lived here her whole life, for reasons he couldn't fathom she wouldn't breach the topic of people's behavior toward her, no matter how hard he prodded. He also found that if he spoke ill of anyone for their behavior, she refused to collaborate. It didn't matter how awkward the situation appeared, Samantha always remained calm and reserved.

Joey came to believe that her way of coping with her strange circumstances was to ignore them. Determined not to jeopardize their friendship, he stopped bringing up the subject when he was around her, although he didn't drop it completely, not until after the incident with his teacher.

That day, he had lingered after class, pretending to organize papers at his desk until he summoned the courage to approach her.

When she had looked up at him, he puffed out his chest and demanded to know why she and the whole town were so cruel to Samantha.

The teacher had given him such a look that the hair on the back of his neck bristled. "We tolerate her the best we can, and she shows us the same courtesy." The teacher looked back down at her book before she continued in a hushed tone, "There is such a thing as bad blood."

Joey had been so jarred by her reaction that he could think of no response. Even though her words didn't explain anything, she had managed to make him feel ashamed for asking, and he had slinked out of the room like he had just been paddled for breaking the rules. He still couldn't meet her gaze when she stood at the front of the class to teach.

The memory sent a chill up his spine, but it also renewed his motivation to keep going. He needed to show Samantha that he could be courageous. He wanted to prove to her that he could save her from this weird town with its winding cobblestone pathways, antique wrought iron lampposts, and crazy superstitions.

"Samantha, I am sorry that I snapped at you. I didn't mean it."

"I know, Joey." Her words came out just above a whisper.

He stopped moving forward and turned to look at her.

Samantha clutched the metal charm around her neck with one hand, as if it would protect her from whatever menacing things loomed in the woods at night. The chain was pulled so taut that it was a wonder it didn't snap in her grip.

Even though Joey had never seen her without the bulky piece of jewelry, it seemed out of place hanging there, especially tonight.

With her light complexion and slight build, she appeared more fragile surrounded by darkness. Yet her eyes seemed to twinkle, as if something else loomed just beneath the surface. A hint of excitement, perhaps, Joey thought.

He reached up and tucked a loose strand of hair behind her ear. Right now, to him she resembled one of the painted porcelain dolls in a toyshop window.

"I can turn the light on, if it would make you feel better."

She lifted her eyebrows, causing her forehead to wrinkle. "It's not that. I can see all right. I have a curfew for a reason. My—"

Joey cut her off. "It's just a bit farther."

She shook her head and grunted before kicking at a loose stone with her foot. "Why do we have to go now? Tonight? I didn't think you would be leading us to the ruins."

He hesitated for a moment then cleared his throat and forced a smile. "Don't tell me you believe the rumors?"

She released the grip on her charm and lowered her eyes.

"Samantha, you're the bravest person I have ever met."

"Do you really think so?" she muttered.

He pushed her chin up and nodded before speaking again. "To face the townspeople over and over has to take courage." Her cheeks colored noticeably, and he prided himself on making her blush.

She opened her mouth as if to speak and then snapped it shut without saying a word.

Knowing that she didn't like to talk about the way the people in town treated her, he cleared his throat and gestured for her to follow.

Before he had a chance to turn away, she reached up and grabbed his arm with her free hand.

Her voice was clearer and much louder as she asked, "Are you sure it's worth it?"

The grip on his arm seemed to tighten with each syllable, and he shook her hand loose, put off by the sudden change in her demeanor.

"It's only been seen during the full moon. Now's our chance to get a peek."

Her eyes latched on to his. "You don't need to prove anything to me."

Afraid his own voice would crack or sound off pitch if he spoke, revealing his returning anxiety, he only nodded before he spun around on his heels so quickly that his shoe hit an exposed root just off the edge of the path, causing him to stumble forward. Although he was relieved that he hadn't landed on his face in front of her, he was too embarrassed to turn back to see if she had noticed his near fall. Instead, he concentrated on keeping his feet within the increasingly uneven path.

A few minutes later, he spotted the first sign that they were nearing the ruins. Long ago, rocks had been piled into mounds around the perimeter, and they still remained, left as a warning to people that traveled through the woods not to venture beyond them, or so he had overheard.

He rushed forward several yards, past a crumbling stone wall, eager to find a place for him and Samantha to hide. Since the trees in this spot were thinned out more, a fair amount of moonlight made its way through the forest canopy, and he placed his hands on his hips to take in the sight in front of him. It was a bit underwhelming.

He had been expecting something more grandiose, from the towns-people's descriptions. A mysterious castle in the woods, perhaps, or an abandoned mansion.

What he found were the remains of two buildings. One was notably smaller than the other, but neither was spectacular in size. To him the larger ruined structure appeared to be nothing more than a dilapidated and overgrown cottage. The roof was missing, as well as much of its external façade, and he could see clear through to the other side. Nearby, the skeletal remains of a second, smaller building protruded from the forest floor, the beams that remained were charcoal black as if they had caught fire at one point.

Neither seemed like an ideal place to hide. Joey made his way back to the stone wall he had passed. It looked like it had once encircled the abandoned property. Now, whole sections had crumbled away, leaving large gaps throughout the waist-high barrier.

"Come on." Joey pointed toward one of the remaining sections. "Let's hide behind that."

Hearing nothing behind him, Joey turned in a circle, scanning the thick woods that surrounded the ruins. "Samantha?" he called out and then listened for the sound of her feet along the trail or the crackling of the undergrowth as she scrambled to catch up, but he heard neither.

Back in his home, such a silence would be tranquil, but out here it was more like the quiet of the graveyard. The thought caused fresh shivers to run up his spine.

He took several steps back the way he had come and then cupped his mouth with his hands before calling to her again. The rustling of leaves could be heard above him, and he glanced skyward as a large bird emerged from the branches of a tree. It let out an annoyed caw as it dove low, coming within inches of him before changing directions and flying back up through the canopy.

Shaken, Joey kept his eyes aimed at the area where the bird had disappeared from view as he took several steps backward. Not watching where he was going, his foot caught on another root. This time he couldn't stop himself from toppling toward a ragged clump of bushes.

Resigned to his fate, he straightened his arms and braced for impact. Several thorns pierced the flesh on his palms as he landed on them, but he clenched his teeth, refusing to let out the strangled cry that rose in his throat.

A giggle that was unmistakably Samantha's seemed to echo all around him as he stood and wiped his bloodied hands against his pant legs. Joey's face burned with embarrassment.

A bit shocked by her behavior, he straightened up and clenched his throbbing hands as he called to her, "This isn't funny."

Spinning on his heels, he turned back in the direction of the ruins. As he did, Samantha emerged from behind a wide tree trunk just off the trail in the distance.

"I'm sorry." She covered her mouth as if to stop another eruption of giggles.

He stomped toward her, his initial shock morphing into anger. "I didn't know if you turned back, got hurt, got lost." He threw his hands up in the air as he stalked past her. "And you were just teasing me the whole time!"

She ran up behind him, and he slowed his steps. His muscles tightened at the feel of her warm hand as it embraced his arm.

"I didn't think you would worry so. I mean, you did tell me I was the bravest person you knew and... Don't tell me that you're worried about the rumors now."

As she slid her hand down his arm and intertwined her fingers with his own, he relaxed. Perhaps his words had made her feel cocky, he thought. He certainly couldn't fault her for that.

Now back within the perimeter of the ruins, he glanced skyward, trying to catch a glimpse of the moon's position, and shrugged. "If we wait much longer to hide, we will probably scare the creature off."

She dropped his hand. "We can't both hide behind that wall."

"Then let's find somewhere else."

"No time. You stay here." She smiled up at him and patted his shoulder. Before he could protest, she turned away and ran farther into the ruins before disappearing behind another short wall.

Alone again, the darkness pressed in on Joey from all sides, and his body screamed for him to run home. Knowing Samantha was probably watching close by, he clenched one of his fists and crouched down behind the strange ruined wall to wait. He closed his eyes and listened for plodding footsteps or the snapping of twigs, but all he heard was the whispering of the light breeze and the faint flutter of wings unseen.

He didn't open them again until a sour smell hit his nose, followed by a burst of warm, moist air. Realizing that he must have dozed momentarily and missed the creature's arrival, he scrambled backward until his body pressed against the barrier of stone.

The ridges bit into his skin as he tried to become one with the wall. But the brittle stones gave out behind him, and he landed on his back. The jagged rocks poked into him hard, causing him to yelp in pain. His heart slammed against his ribs as he gulped at the air.

He made a conscious effort to try to slow his breathing enough to focus on the rest of the world around him. Above him was a mass of teeth and fur.

The thing turned up its face to the moon and howled.

When it lowered its snout again, Joey could see that its ears were pulled back and its lips were tucked up, revealing long, sharp teeth.

He reached out across the ground with one hand in search of his flashlight, but as he moved forward, the wolf's hackles raised, and deep rumbles came from its throat.

Joey felt a warm dampness spread across the front of his jeans.

The wolf's head lowered slightly, causing droplets of saliva to drip from its mouth. Its nostrils flared as it seemed to breathe in his scent.

He forced himself to reach out again, feeling with his fingers. As they skimmed the small end of the flashlight's smooth surface, he hesitated, aware that in seconds his throat could be ripped out and his flesh consumed. He gulped, dreading his next move, but knowing he had to try to get away, if only to make sure Samantha was safe.

According to the rumors, the beast wasn't a wild animal at all but a werewolf. He hadn't believed the stories—not really. Now, when faced with the monster, he couldn't help but wonder if it was true. Surely a wild animal would have torn him to shreds by now. He could only hope to startle it long enough to make his move.

"Don't eat me!" he blurted as he reached out for the hefty flashlight. He didn't dare take his eyes off the creature as his fingers curled around it, searching for the button. There was a soft click as he found the oval shape and pressed in. He kept the light lowered and took a deep breath.

To his surprise, the monstrosity began to back up slowly. When it stopped, its ears pricked up, and it cocked its head to the side. He watched, shocked by the change, as it lifted its tail and began to wag it back and forth.

Taking the behavior as a good sign but still trembling, Joey pushed himself up onto his feet and lifted the torch toward the monster. The beam illuminated the wolf's muscular, fur-covered body as it lowered its tail and again turned its face skyward to release another howl.

A shimmer caught Joey's eye as the light hit something around its neck. When it lowered its face, their gazes locked. He wrinkled his brow in confusion as he wiped his tear-stained cheeks with the back of his free hand.

Stammering, he managed to whisper, "Samantha? Is that you?"

Her whole body seemed to tense back up with his words. Her ears flattened back against her head, and a low, warning growl arose from her throat. Joey let the flashlight drop from his hand. Before it hit the ground, she lunged at him, knocking him back down onto the crumbled stones.

The Warning

From the moment May first stood before it, she thought, *That's a creepy old house.* "Historic" was how her parents referred to it. It didn't help that beside the house was a large hollowed-out oak. The monstrosity loomed over the house, preventing light from entering the large windows. Its gnarled branches reached in every direction.

No grass could be seen growing underneath, because all sunlight was completely blocked by its outstretched limbs, and in some places the tree's thick roots protruded back up out of the ground, waiting for the chance to trip up an unsuspecting visitor as they made their way to the door.

She wondered what type of creature lived in the hole at the base. The cavity didn't look natural to her; deep marks could be seen around its edges, as if a creature had dug into the trunk purposefully, and she thought maybe a gnome or a small goblin resided inside.

The front of the house appeared to be grinning. The porch stretched its full length with dead vines snaking their way up the old lattice on each side, which added to the effect. A balcony centered directly above jutted out like a wide nose. Two windows on either side were slightly elevated, just enough to give the appearance of eyes.

She shuddered as she imagined it chewing up anyone that dared to enter and spitting the remains back out into the hedges that lined the front yard. The hair on her arms prickled, and she folded them over her chest as she glanced at her smiling sister.

Butterflies took flight in May's stomach, and she let out a low groan. She couldn't understand why Elisa looked so ecstatic about the move. They had always been close, even though her sister was four years older, or at least up until a few weeks ago when she had started high school. Now it felt to May like she barely knew her anymore.

Elisa was excited when she saw the house for the first time. She had already been looking forward to living in town, where she would be closer to her friends. Then, as she stood before it, marveling at how much more space they would have, her parents announced that she would get first choice of the bedrooms, since she was older. Elisa couldn't help but smile from ear to ear. She knew exactly what room she wanted, and she couldn't wait to get inside to unpack.

Over the past few weeks, her parents had described the house and shown them a few pictures of the interior. They had mentioned a bedroom on the upper floor that was separated from all the rest by a bathroom that split the long main hallway. It seemed perfect, even before they revealed the fact that it had an entirely separate staircase, which led right up to it from the kitchen.

The additional privacy sounded pretty appealing to her. It would put a little extra space between her and her sister's overactive imagination. It wasn't that she found her behavior annoying, but they did enjoy different things, and although Elisa was admittedly the more rambunctious of the two, her sister could be rather melodramatic and, in her opinion, immature at times. In fact, when she had stopped inviting her along to hang out with her friends, May had accused her of being a pod person, amongst other things.

Elisa didn't have the heart to tell May that it was mainly because her friends had started making comments about the way May always seemed to finish her sentences, like she knew exactly what she was thinking. Elisa glanced over at her sister, and her smile faltered. She seemed terrified.

Her first instinct was to approach and console May, but Elisa fought it. She couldn't expect her sister to act more mature if she always rushed to her side.

She assured herself that once May spent some time in the house, maybe a night or two in her new room, she would get over whatever fearful thing her brain had conjured up.

The first time May heard the voice calling to her, it had sounded low, strained, almost inaudible. She hadn't dared to close her eyes and was too frightened to look anywhere but at the ceiling. "Help me," the words came again. She wanted to run but felt stuck to the bed, as if her blanket had somehow transformed into masking tape.

Stricken with paralyzing fear, she strained her ears as she tried to determine its source, but she couldn't tell if the noise was coming from somewhere in the hall or if the offender was inside her room. Not even a speck of light shined in through her window. The moon's position caused its glow to be blocked by the branches of that old oak.

"Help me," the guttural sound repeated, louder. Closer.

May swore she could feel each tiny hair on her neck prickle one by one. The seconds ticked by like hours as she lay there, tormented by the increasing volume of the repetitive noise. The feeling of dread at the pit of her stomach seemed to creep up into her throat.

Although panic filled her, she didn't want to scream. Her parents would never believe her if she told them about the voice; they had already accused her of creating otherworldly hoaxes throughout the house. Her mom even threatened to take her books away, blaming her increasing anxiety on the intensity of their contents, when in fact they were her only escape from it.

She held the scream in by biting down on the sides of her tongue a little too hard, causing her mouth to fill with the iron taste of blood.

There was only one chance for salvation she could think of, but she wasn't sure her sister would welcome her if she managed to make the trek. She had barely spoken to May over the past few days. It seemed like she was avoiding her.

Her heart pounded in her ears, but even so, when the voice came again, she swore it was followed by the faintest shuffling somewhere close by.

She clenched her fists under the covers to try to subdue the shaking of her hands. Whether Elisa turned her away or not, she had to get out of this room.

Counting to herself and working up the nerve to move, she suddenly sat upright and leapt out of bed. May was careful not to look anywhere but straight ahead as she ran from the dark room, sure she would see a ghoul or some other aberration ready to pounce if she did.

Once she made it to the safety of the bathroom that split the hall, she turned on the light and splashed water on her face, as if she was trying to wash away the memory of that eerie voice.

She spun around with a start as a blurred image appeared in the mirror behind her. Her mouth fell open as the thing reached out to her, touching her shoulder. It took a moment for her mind to catch up. Luckily, something registered before she could find her voice and cry out.

Her sister placed a finger over her lips and shook her head before reaching for her hand.

Still trembling with fear, May accepted it and allowed Elisa to pull her into her room.

Only when her door was firmly closed did Elisa speak, whispering so quietly that May had a hard time understanding.

"Did you hear it?"

May only nodded in response. Her older sister's whispers were somehow even more chilling than the voice had been, and she realized she didn't feel any safer in here with Elisa.

It probably didn't help that there was a door in the ceiling that led up to the attic, which always seemed to emit the soft swoosh sound of air being forced around. The effect caused May to imagine that it was the house itself breathing slowly in and out.

Apart from that, the room featured just one tiny, solitary window, which had been nailed shut by the previous owners and a separate staircase that led directly down to the kitchen.

That dark stairway gave May goose bumps just thinking about it. Halfway down the steps there was a single bulb always swaying. It was unable to light the winding staircase adequately, and shadows constantly moved along the walls. The whole setup made her feel cut off and isolated, but she would stay if her sister would allow her to.

Elisa was relieved as she placed a pillow and blanket on the floor for her younger sister. She didn't want to be alone with her thoughts, and allowing her to stay eased some of the guilt she felt for ignoring her.

Knowing that May would appreciate the soft glow of the light, she clicked on her lava lamp and watched in silence as her sister obediently laid in the bed she had created for her.

Earlier, when Elisa had been awakened by the voice, she had sprung from her mattress to find the source. She enjoyed a good mystery, even if it took place in the dead of night, and she hadn't had much of an opportunity to indulge in such frivolous entertainments since she had been distancing herself from her sister. She missed spending time with May, and she regretted the way she had been treating her.

As she had crossed her room and the sound repeated, she realized that the words were traveling through the heating vent.

Thinking that perhaps her younger sister was playing a prank on her by talking through the vent in her own room in an attempt to get her attention, Elisa had decided to confront her and maybe share a laugh.

Not wanting to wake her parents, she tiptoed through the bathroom and down the long hallway, past their closed door. All the while, she continued to hear the voice, and it seemed to be getting louder as she approached her sister's open door. She peeked her head around the frame. The room was dark, but she could make out the bulge of her sister's form under the blankets. Elisa furrowed her brow.

Disconcerted, she began tiptoeing back toward her own room to mull it over. She had just about made it into her bed when she heard her sister's frantic footsteps coming down the hall in her direction.

Although the look of terror on May's face when she had approached her in the bathroom had reinforced Elisa's new theory that she had nothing to do with the voice, as the initial shock wore off and she reminded herself that there was most likely a logical explanation for what they had heard, she couldn't help but question the other strange things that had happened over the last few days.

Elisa chewed thoughtfully at her bottom lip. Since they had moved in, May had been blamed for quite a few pranks. Like her parents, Elisa had been quick to assume her sister was the culprit, even though she had never done anything like it before.

They all knew May wasn't happy about the move, so when things appeared repacked in boxes after having been neatly put away and the skeleton keys for the bedroom doors vanished, she seemed to be the logical suspect. Her insistence that it was something inhuman was disregarded as an invention of her large imagination to cover up the crimes.

Now, she couldn't deny the possibility that her sister could have been innocent all along. A shiver ran up her spine, and she pulled her blanket tight around her shoulders.

Elisa muttered as she scolded herself for letting her imagination run wild.

She glanced down at May, and seeing that she had fallen asleep, Elisa closed her eyes in an attempt to do the same. It had been a while since she heard the eerie sound rising up from her vent anyway, and she assured herself, they would have all weekend to uncover the mysterious source of the events after they got some rest.

Sleep came only in tiny chunks as she tossed and turned. The room was hot and seemed to be getting warmer by the minute. If she didn't know better, she would have thought someone had filled the furnace with wood and set it ablaze. That was something her father wouldn't do until after the first frost, and it was still early fall. The leaves had barely begun changing color.

Not yet willing to give up the battle, she pushed her blanket to the side and wiped the sweat from her brow. Wishing that she had pried out the nails that were hammered into the frame of her window, she released a frustrated huff.

Soon after, a soft mewling began to rise up from the floor. Elisa let out another huff as she popped her eyes open and sat up. The sound was coming from May. She was sitting up with her arms locked around her legs, pulling her knees to her chest as she stared toward the window. Elisa turned to follow her gaze, and her breath caught in her throat.

Perfectly framed by the window, the boy just outside it looked like an underdeveloped Polaroid. Semitransparent red and orange flames encircled his image as small pieces of him seemed to flicker in and out of sight.

Elisa swore she could feel the heat of the fire that surrounded his shape and hear the faintest crackling, yet his clothing, which resembled some type of uniform, appeared unmarred.

Curiously, although he held a baseball in one hand, which was outstretched in their direction, to Elisa it looked like the ghostly apparition's pale blue eyes stared past her and May. She reached a shaky hand out and placed it on May's shoulder trying to get her attention, but her sister didn't turn to look back at her.

It felt like an eternity passed while she waited for something to happen, but both her sister and the vision remained unchanged up until the moment it vanished from sight. When it did, her sister turned to face her with eyes as round as saucers.

Elisa stood, lifting her hand from her sister's shoulder as she moved toward the window.

When she peered out into the empty, moonlit backyard, she felt May move up beside her and reach for her hand. She gave it a gentle, reassuring squeeze as she accepted it into her own.

Below in the dark backyard she thought she saw the faintest movement, but it was hard to focus on the spot. She reasoned that perhaps it was an illusion caused by staring too long into the almost featureless beyond, but then she saw it again.

Her grip tightened in panic as something white came hurling toward them from outside. Elisa tugged her sister backward just as it collided, making a thwack sound as it struck. She watched for a split-second as the glass cracked, spiderwebbing outward from the window's center, then yanked her sister from the room.

The back staircase seemed dark and ominous. Thinking that the bulb that hung from its ceiling had gone out, she bypassed it without a second thought.

She didn't stop moving until they had made it through the bathroom and all the way down the hall. Her heart pounded as she stopped at the top of the main staircase. There, she shook her sister's hand loose and motioned for her to follow as she began a slow descent to the lower level. The downstairs was open and well lit. It felt like a better place to wait out the dawn.

Her younger sister stuck to her side as she made her rounds, flicking on the light switches one by one. She was no longer worried about the consequences of waking her parents; her cracked window was proof enough that something had happened, although what exactly, she wasn't sure.

As she reached for the last switch, she heard another loud thwack, followed by the sound of cracking glass, as something came into contact with a window nearby.

Elisa pulled May close and sank down onto the carpeted floor. Even while holding her sister in a tight hug, she couldn't stop herself from flinching as the sound came again from the direction of a different window. Elisa squeezed her eyes shut.

May's pajamas were soaked through with sweat when she sat up in her bed. Her lips tightened and stretched horizontally. It had been so real, the voice, the boy, everything, but she didn't remember returning to her room, and she doubted that her sister was strong enough to carry her back upstairs. There was no way that it had all been a dream.

"Elisa." The name sounded more like the croaking of a frog as she jumped up from her bed and proceeded to run as fast as she could through the hall. She collided painfully with her sister at the entrance to the bathroom. Unfazed, she took two quick steps back before blurting her question: "Did you bring me up to bed?"

Elisa shook her head then whispered, "I don't think so."

May's eyebrows drew together as she folded her arms over her chest and squeaked out, "But you were there, you saw it too?"

Instead of answering, Elisa spun away from her, moving back into the bathroom, where she grabbed two washcloths and ran cold water over them. One was for her sister's tear-streaked face, and the other was for her painful swollen lip. May had slammed into her so hard that she had bitten into it, drawing blood.

She pressed one of the damp cloths against her throbbing mouth and held the other out to May. A scowl spread on her sister's face as she snatched it from her hand.

Elisa spoke in a hushed tone as she beckoned May to enter the room. "I saw...something."

To Elisa it looked like May deflated as she dropped her arms to her sides before crossing the threshold. Once she was in the room, Elisa shut and locked both doors. She understood her sister's confusion all too well.

Earlier, when she had opened her eyes to see the familiar light purple paint that decorated her walls, Elisa had felt disoriented. The last thing she remembered was being in the living room with her sister held tightly in her arms, yet when she sat up and threw her legs over the edge of her mattress, the pillow and blanket she remembered setting up for May earlier in the evening were nowhere to be seen. If she hadn't gotten out of bed and noticed the cracked window and the blown-out bulb on the back stairwell, she could have shrugged off the whole experience.

"Can two people have the same dream, Elisa?" May's voice cracked.

She had sunk down into a sitting position on the cold linoleum tiles, and Elisa joined her there.

"I don't know."

She wrapped an arm around May's back as she added, "Maybe we should compare what we remember?"

May gave her a slow nod in response.

Signaling that it was 5:00 a.m., the shrill beeping of their father's alarm clock interrupted the girls' storytelling. May welcomed the sound. She had grown tired of rehashing the events, although she did feel better knowing that Elisa had experienced things in exactly the same way she had, because it meant someone knew she wasn't making it all up.

She imitated her sister as she pushed herself up from the floor and moved toward the sink to inspect herself in the mirror. She combed down her messy hair as Elisa pinched at her cheeks, trying to add a bit of pinkness to them. May didn't think the grooming helped at all. Side by side, their reflections still looked pale and ragged.

Their father rarely slept in on the weekends, so it wasn't surprising when they heard him make his way out into the hall and head toward the stairs.

The girls quietly crept out of the room and began to follow.

As he reached the stairwell, they heard him grumble about electricity and lights, no doubt thinking she was playing another prank, but his complaint was cut short as he neared the bottom step. His hands went to his hips as a low whistling sound escaped his mouth.

He must have heard their approaching footsteps, because he turned his face up toward them on the landing and said, "Don't look out there." He made a sweeping motion toward the cracked window, then spun on his heels and quickly made his way around the corner, out of sight.

May glanced up at Elisa and then continued to move down the stairs. Despite her father's warning, she turned to look out the window as she neared it. She released a startled gasp as she viewed the owl that lay unmoving on the ground just below the frame. She knew that birds sometimes flew into closed windows during the day due to reflections in the glass, but she had never seen it occur, nor had she heard of it happening at night.

She felt Elisa place a hand on her shoulder and allowed herself to be steered away from the sight. Her dad had been rummaging in the kitchen for something, and he must have found it, because she heard the back door close with a bang as he exited the house.

A few rays of dawn's earliest light managed to strike the picture window that stretched across the dining room wall, drawing the girls' attention to it. Here the glass appeared to have spiderwebbed up and out from the lower right-hand corner, instead of at dead center as the previous two had been.

While looking through the window, May caught a glimpse of her father carrying a garbage bag into the detached garage before turning back to the house. She cast her eyes toward the ground, but whatever had struck the window had already been removed.

The kitchen door banged again as their father reentered the house. Although clearly annoyed at the prospect of replacing windows, he pasted a smile on his face as he approached. "You two are up early."

Elisa began wringing her hands together nervously as she spoke. "My window..."

His smile dropped in disbelief. "Another one?"

Elisa lowered her voice noticeably as she continued, "I heard something hit it. I caught a glimpse of feathers but hadn't been able to bring myself to step closer..."

His face turned a deep red, and May could hear him muttering under his breath as he swiftly moved toward the kitchen and then bounded up the back staircase, apparently unfazed by their gloominess.

Before their mother appeared to prepare breakfast, Elisa had instructed her sister to keep quiet about their experience. She knew that if she hadn't gone through it as well, she never would have believed it happened, but she soon found that she had trouble heeding her own advice. Each time she noticed the irritated look on her father's face, she had to bite her tongue, which made breakfast a silent and uncomfortable affair. She wanted to tell him everything; it made her feel helpless, and she wondered if May had felt that way all along.

They had just about finished their meal when the urgent steady beeping of the fire alarm reached her ears. The look on her father's face morphed from irritation to alarm as he ushered everyone outside, the broken windows forgotten.

Elisa tried to push the memory of the night's events out of her mind as she waited with her family at the end of their winding driveway, but try as she might, her thoughts kept returning to them.

As she looked over at the front of the old house, goose bumps formed on her arms, and she felt the hair on the back of her neck prickle up.

She swore the house was grinning back at her.

May was glad that her sister had stopped ignoring her after the fire. In fact, she felt like they had grown even closer than before. She reached for her sister's hand and clasped it firmly. She knew Elisa was nervous about returning to her room. She had told her as much after their parents had read the inspector's report.

Elisa was having a hard time believing that faulty wires in her wall had caused the blaze, and try as she might, May had been unable to convince her of it over the past few weeks.

As their parents appeared on the front porch and waved to them to come inside and see the newly remodeled rooms, the color drained from her older sister's face. "What about the things we saw and heard May?"

"I told you, it was a warning, Elisa." She had explained this to her older sister before, to try to quell her newfound anxiety about the house, but it never seemed to help.

"I'm not so sure about that."

May gave her sister's hand another squeeze. "The dream saved you."

She tried to sound reassuring as she added, "If you would have slept in, you could have burned up in your bed."

"Please, don't remind me," Elisa whispered.

Thinking her older sister was acting a little immature, May tugged at her arm to get her moving. She figured after spending a night or two back in her room, she would get over whatever fearful thing her brain had conjured up.

The Felling

On the morning the trees came down, they made a sound. A dry thud against the earth. It was what she had expected. What happened next, though, as the roots came up, dragging with them those entangled remains of the past, the noise that accompanied them echoed so loudly, it was almost unbearable.

Jillian didn't know why she was the only one that could hear them, but it was obvious that no one else did, or their reactions wouldn't have been so impassive.

She had been watching from the kitchen window the whole time, unable to pull her eyes from the sight. Her coffee cup had long stopped feeling warm against her palm. Still, she cradled the bottom with one hand and clutched the handle with the other.

Those bones, even though devoid of life and personality at the time, had screamed out as they were released from their prison, causing her to drop the cup. She had trembled as she stared at the broken pieces and the brown liquid that had splattered in every direction.

It should have brought her peace, being rid of them. It didn't... The truth of what they had dredged up from the past was much worse than anything she had imagined, and she couldn't expect the detective to understand.

Even now that they were no longer simply bones, in a manner of speaking, the screaming still hadn't stopped.

"Jillian, do you know why I asked you to come in and make another statement?"

She had been expecting the call, but she shook her head anyway and answered, "I just assume that you had follow-up questions regarding the bones that were found in my yard."

"Yes, well, it's a tad more complicated than that. We last interviewed you on, let's see here, Monday the 17th? Does that sound right?"

She nodded.

"The paperwork says that they took your statement at your home?"

"Yes. That's right."

"But your husband was unavailable?"

"He had to leave town that Sunday evening. He had an early-morning investment meeting."

"Does he take business trips a lot?"

"Quite a bit. Once or twice a month."

He reached into his leather briefcase and produced a yellow piece of paper that he slid toward her. She recognized it as the work order she had signed for the arborist on the morning of the event. As she was looking the document over, he slid a copy of her marriage license beside it.

Confused, she looked up at him. "What's this for?"

He pointed at the yellow page, then the photocopy. "Why do you think that your signature is barely legible on this newer document?"

"Because I was in a hurry to sign it. I was still in my robe when they got there."

"Are you sure that you weren't shaking? Emotional? Because that's how the crew described you."

"Of course I was emotional; they found three people's bones in my yard."

"I am referring to the morning before the work began."

"They thought my behavior was off? What about theirs? They barely flinched when they pulled those bones up from the ground."

"It's not uncommon to find bones."

"Human?"

He waved a hand in the air as if dismissing the comment. "That point is moot, unless they approached you to remove the trees instead of the other way around, which is not the case, so it hardly matters. They followed procedure. I am asking about *you*."

He lifted his brows at her accusingly. "Did you know about the bodies before you scheduled the felling?"

When she didn't answer right away, he leaned in toward her from across the interrogation room table, and she could smell coffee, cigarettes, and sweat.

"No."

"Then why did you insist on it being done, Jillian?" He cocked his eyebrows at her and sneered.

She caught sight of the grime on his yellowed teeth and pulled her eyes away, back down to the tabletop where her hands were folded.

Why? That was a fair question, she supposed. Having those trees removed was an expense they didn't need to bear, and yet she had pushed the issue. She had just wanted them gone.

Without those pines, the yard was bright, welcoming, almost cheerful. Filled with flowers and other plants, brimming. But those two trees had elicited a sense of foreboding within her that she hadn't been able to shake after they moved in. In fact, as the years passed, that feeling had only gotten stronger. She hadn't known the reasons, at least not until the crew uprooted them.

She kept her voice low. "I just wanted more room in the yard."

"You didn't have the slightest idea?" he prodded, still not budging from his aggressive position.

Jillian shook her head and closed her eyes. He would never believe her if she told him about the intense feelings the trees caused her. She spoke with as much conviction as she could muster. "Of course not. How would I?"

He remained where he was, the look on his face unchanged. Jillian could hear him breathing. Each time he inhaled deeply, the rough, lungy breath would be accompanied by a soft wheeze. The sounds were louder she thought, than they should have been, and she wondered if he was coming down with something or if years of smoking had taken a toll on him.

She opened her eyes and looked back up into his. He was relentless. She doubted he would stop unless she tried harder to explain. "We moved in a few years ago."

Jillian paused, and although he managed to do it without breaking eye contact, she was relieved as she watched him slither back down into his seat. She unfolded her hands and began to fiddle with her wedding band. "They gave me the creeps." She muttered the words as if ashamed to admit her qualm. She hoped that the honesty in the statement would help convince him. There were odd moments when from a distance the pine trees had looked beautiful, even downright majestic while covered with a sprinkling of snow and such, but they usually just gave her the willies.

"What?" The single-word question sprang from his mouth as if what she said was just as incriminating as her silence.

She steadied her voice and raised it an octave. "Those trees gave me the creeps."

"So, you *are* saying that you had reason to suspect?"

She shook her head and looked away again. "I am only saying that my husband promised we would remove them, and I had been patient. I tried waiting for what he considered to be the right time, and the right time was never going to come. So I went ahead and hired someone to do it while he would be out of town."

He slapped one of his hands down on the table, glowing as if what she said had somehow made things clearer.

She stiffened and furrowed her brow as she wondered what he thought he knew. Nothing, she reassured herself. He was just grasping at straws, poking around like detectives did on television. She relaxed her body. He couldn't possibly know the truth. He was just looking for holes in her story and trying to find somewhere to place blame.

She wondered if it would do more harm to push him in the right direction. She certainly didn't have anything else to lose.

She was careful to keep her voice even as she asked, "Just what are you getting at? Those trees have had to have been there a long time. They could have been planted shortly after the house was built." She cocked one of her eyebrows. "I believe the previous owners planted them, directly above the corpses."

He nodded in acknowledgement of her words before speaking. "On that we can agree."

She countered, this time failing to keep her voice steady. "So go after *them* and stop grilling me!"

"Don't you think it's odd that you insisted on having them removed when your husband is on the brink of losing his business?"

"I thought that I made it clear that I just couldn't stand them anymore."

"So you are claiming to be a psychic? Is that it?"

The word resonated with her. She had never thought about it like that before. Perhaps she thought instead of being sensitive to the dead, she could only feel the undead. A skill that could come in handy if it had been and was in fact still true. Even if it was, she certainly couldn't offer that excuse to him.

She let out a nervous giggle as she shook her head and rolled her eyes. "I have never sensed anything else like it," she lied. "It was just a feeling. I don't know how I can explain it."

"Try."

She tilted her head to the side as she attempted to get him to understand her reasoning with a less fantastical explanation than the one she had just considered. "Did you notice the bright rowan bushes on the other side of the lawn?"

He nodded, a questioning gleam in his eyes.

"It's summer, and those small shrubs were full of white berries, yet there were no birds. There are never any birds, unless you count the occasional crow."

He sat forward. "What are you getting at? Are you saying the birds knew something was buried in your yard?"

She shrugged. "You tell me. You're the detective. If you saw that flower-filled lawn day after day and never saw a squirrel, a bird, or a rabbit, wouldn't you think something was off?"

He lifted a finger in her direction, shaking it at her. "You planted those flowers."

She shook her head again. "No. We just mowed the lawn in between the patches of flowers. The arrangement of the beds appeared so well done that we left them just as the previous homeowners had kept them."

"And the crucifixes?"

Jillian smirked at him. She knew that the crosses had been found buried beneath the soil at different levels, throughout the yard. "Not mine ether."

She lifted the warm paper cup and pretended to sip the flavorless drink he had given her when she first arrived.

"Unbelievable." The word seemed to wheeze out of him as if he was a punctured balloon. His shoulders slumped and he shook his head. "Have you been back to the house?"

She started to shake her head, then recanted. The smirk dissolved from her face before she spoke. "I did go back, after I got word that the heads had been located and removed, to see if my husband had shown up. But I'm not staying there now."

He paused to roll up his sleeves before asking the next question. "And did you see your husband at all?"

"Not since he first returned from his trip and found out about the digging. Surely you don't think he knew?"

He produced a manila envelope and slid it toward her. "He never put his name on the transfer documents."

She smacked her lips as she spoke up in his defense. "That's because I used a small inheritance to buy the house outright. I came into it shortly before we started looking, and it was just enough to cover the asking price and closing costs. There was no need for a loan."

He pulled a pen from his breast pocket and jotted something on a notepad that until then had lain blank on the tabletop. When he finished writing, he dropped the pen next to the pad and tilted his face in her direction. "Why aren't you cooperating?"

"I am. It seems to me that you are the one that isn't being upfront about what you want."

"Fine. Let me ask you this then." He leaned in toward her again and locked his eyes on hers. "Do you think your husband took the bodies from the morgue?"

The look of shock on her face was authentic; she had known the remains had disappeared from the morgue, but she never thought that the detective would accuse her poor husband.

"When did that happen? Never mind. It doesn't matter. Absolutely not." She said it with conviction, but she didn't rightly know how the process worked.

She only assumed that when the mortician had matched the heads with the bones, the corpses had been revived. She figured that like her, her husband was dead, just more permanently so.

She looked down at her hands, again, biting at her lower lip with her front teeth as it quivered.

Her husband was historically even more stubborn than she was. He probably didn't tell the vampires what they needed to hear. She picked up the cup once more and imitated sipping. She didn't want to think about the details of what could have happened. Her own encounter with them had been rather civil, for the most part.

The detective slammed both hands down onto the table in frustration. "But you haven't seen him, so how can you be so sure? Maybe he knew the previous owners, and he was helping them conceal their crimes."

She gasped at his words. As it was, she felt guilty for insisting that her husband meet her at the house at all. She had shown up an hour later than she agreed, just because she had been angry at him. By then, as far as she knew, he was no longer there.

She hadn't thought to ask the trio of visitors that she found waiting in his place about his whereabouts.

It wasn't the way they looked that unsettled her, since they seemed to be as normal as any other nuclear family she had encountered. It was the reoccurrence of the unease that she had until then, only experienced around those two pine trees.

What other choice was there, but to listen to what they had to say and answer their questions as best she could?

It wasn't until after they had learned all they believed they could from her that the mother figure, who introduced herself as Lillian, had revealed her fangs and thanked her for the part she played in releasing them from their graves.

Startling her from her thoughts, the officer broke the persistent silence by asking her once more if she was sure that she hadn't seen her husband since his initial return and Jillian wondered if it would benefit her to mention their visit. Surely, if he managed to find them, they would get rid of him.

She let out a sigh. "If you must know, I left him a message to meet me, but he never showed. Probably because he was upset with me when I told him that I wanted to sell the house." She paused and then added reassuringly. "After the investigation is complete, of course. I just don't want to live there, not after…well, you know. And like you pointed out, it's my property. He doesn't really get a say. Not anymore."

"So your time at home was uneventful, nothing happened?"

"There was one thing. I doubt it's important."

"I will be the one to determine what's important and what's not."

"I got a visit that day while I waited. To be honest, they seemed like a nice enough family. They asked me about Marilee." She explained, "That would be the previous owner's name."

He nodded, and she smiled timidly at him.

"Anyway, they said she was a relative and that she had been estranged from the family for a while. They asked me if I knew whether or not her significant other was still alive. Apparently, he had been the cause of their falling out."

"Did they say anything else, their names perhaps?"

"The matriarch introduced herself as Lillian Elliot. The other two didn't say much. I mean, they really didn't stay long. I couldn't rightly answer their questions, after all. The property transfer was handled by lawyers."

She stared at the pulsating vein in his neck. Her stomach rumbled, and she hoped he didn't hear it. She began to chew at her lower lip once again, she just had to hold it together a few more minutes so she could wrap this up and hopefully deter the detective from bothering her further, without a more justifiable cause.

They told her it was a prize for being cooperative, but she had seen enough vampire movies to know that they wanted to keep her walking the earth, in case they found out she had been deceiving them and wanted to find her again to punish her further.

She tightened the scarf around her neck. At the spot where Lillian had penetrated her flesh with her teeth days ago, the wound remained. Two empty gaping punctures that she reasoned probably wouldn't close until she gave in to her desire and fed for the first time.

She had to get away from him before it was too late. She cleared her throat noisily. "Speaking of lawyers, perhaps I should call mine and see what she makes of all this?"

"I don't think that's necessary."

"Then I have to go.

"What's your rush?"

"Rush?" She raised her voice higher, yelling for the first time. "I have been here all night, and I need to get some sleep."

Obviously taken aback by her outburst, he stammered, "If you would have shown up earlier in the day…"

She raised her hand in a gesture to silence him as she stood knocking her chair backward loudly. "It's obvious that you have no reason to hold me."

This time she leaned against the table and looked him in the eye, causing him to lean back in his chair and gape at her with wide eyes.

"Or do you?"

"What if your husband decides to forgive you for your decision and shows up?"

She shrugged and grinned at him, not caring if the tips of her fangs showed. "He shouldn't have any trouble finding me, and I will be sure to let you know if he does."

He stared back at her in stunned silence. The color had drained from his face.

She stood upright and smoothed down her dress as she composed herself. "Now that it's all settled, I will be going."

Dead Already

I think you slowly forget as you go on after death, and that's why Becky no longer speaks to me. Instead, she only motions senselessly and moans. Her ghostly cries can be heard from outside, echoing through the walls of the house, and I wish it would stop.

I haven't always been able to hear her, but I remember the first time I did.

I came to the conclusion a while back that I must have been unconscious for a time. The day leading up to it is a puzzle. Nothing more to me now than a sequence of blurry snapshots taken with instant film that never developed properly.

What transpired after I came to is still quite clear.

I could feel the cold edge of the claw-foot tub beneath my throbbing skull. I had tried to lift it, to look up. But my neck refused to bear its weight, and I only managed to rock it from side to side enough to cause my chin to fall forward onto my chest.

As my limp body shifted, sinking lower in the bath, the red-tinged water inched up toward my face.

Barry had hunched down low over the tub and thrust his arm into the water beside me. I tried to dodge away, but no matter how much I urged it, my body refused to move any farther. I watched helplessly as he fumbled beneath my torso to pull the drain stopper out.

When the water began to gurgle and splash around me, he lifted it triumphantly in his hand. At that moment when his icy blue eyes locked with mine, that was when her sobbing cries of warning had filled my ears.

I had been startled, to say the least. In fact, if I still had the ability, I probably would have jolted upright and lifted my hand to my chest as I myself cried out in shock.

Those screams, those cries of warning and terror, were the first things I heard as the pain from my throbbing head vanished.

Did I know he was going to kill me? That's the question, isn't it? There were signs, I guess. Things I didn't notice or blew off. Incidents I chose to ignore.

I suppose I didn't know enough about the world and relationships when I entered this one.

I certainly didn't see my future as lying limp in his creepy old claw-foot bathtub, lips blue and skin pale.

I am not sure how long he left my body there. I watched myself for what seemed like weeks, but it couldn't have been. Time moves strangely for me now. At some moments it seems to slow down to a crawl, while at others it seems to speed up as if someone hit fast-forward on an old video cassette player.

I think for the unliving, that's just the way time works.

An uncontrollable moan escaped me when I watched him lift my newly dressed body from the tub. You see, until that moment I hadn't realized that I was no longer looking up at him, but rather at the same level. What was worse, the thing that had caused the outburst was that I could see myself cradled in his arms.

I watched him carry my spiritless body down the cement cellar stairs, and I lashed out at him, screaming. For a moment I thought he had heard me as he turned toward my apparition with a jerk and began mumbling to himself.

But he had simply forgotten to flick the light on, and I just happened to be hovering in front of the switch.

It was difficult to watch as he gently laid my broken body into the cavity that he had created within the cement floor. I clenched my fists and cringed as he smoothed my skirt and brushed the hair from my pale face.

I noticed his cheeks were tear-streaked as he leaned over my body to give my blue lips a kiss. But those tears quickly dried as he dumped scoopfuls of lye into the hole with the ease of desalting the driveway.

He finished his project by covering my remains with a thin sheet of plastic and a few buckets of freshly mixed cement.

Whether upset or just worn out by his chore, he laid his head there beside his worksite on the dirty cement floor and fell asleep.

I stayed close by him the first few days after the burial. I followed him around as he emptied my things from the closets into boxes and bags for storage.

I couldn't help but wonder how long it would be before people realized I was gone. I had been cut off from my friends and family for so long, I wasn't even sure that they would notice. People will only go so far to try to stay in touch before they get fed up with declined invitations and unanswered phone calls.

How long had she been warning me?

Since the first time I stepped into that house, of this I am certain.

Her warning had fallen on deaf ears until it was too late. Thinking back, I know now that I had felt her, sensed her presence, even seen her once before I died. I just didn't realize what I was experiencing.

It was by the sunflowers that surround the porch. A trick of the sun, I thought. A shimmer from the heat followed by the murmur of the wind. It gave me chills, but I shook it off.

Of course I did.

You see, it had indeed been a hot day. Record-breaking, if memory serves me. But I had become newly unemployed at Barry's request and was still adjusting to the schedule change.

So I sat out under that hot sun for most of the afternoon, trimming hedges and planting flowers along the back of the house.

By the time the dizziness from the exposure hit, I was unable to make it back to the front door.

It wasn't until Barry returned from the office where we had once both worked that he had lifted my collapsed form up from the lawn.

And when I saw that shimmering outline as my savior helped me inside, I couldn't acknowledge it for what it truly was.

Don't make the same mistake I did.

When you sit on the couch with your book propped in your lap, do you feel me as I read over your shoulder?

I think you do.

I see how you pull the blanket up wrapping it tightly around your shoulders after I enter the room and how you look up suddenly each time I try to murmur in your ear.

Not my cup of tea, those vampire stories, but it's not like I have many options for reading material anymore.

It helps to save me from complete boredom at least.

Boredom?

Yes, ghosts get it to. I quickly became restless after Becky lost her ability to roam around the inside of the house.

She seems to be almost rooted to that area by the front porch.

Molly, you have to understand that I am not trying to scare you. I realize simply freaking you out would do no good. I was restless, and I needed a purpose, anything to do besides having strange games of charades with the remnants of Becky.

I have always wanted to help her, but I didn't know how.

And then you showed up.

And I had to show you that you were in danger.

I hope you can understand that I had to take action now, while I am able to go where I like and while I still have the ability to communicate.

I can see her fading day by day, and so I know my time is not infinite.

I must tell you as my memories come to me, since I'm not sure what will fade first. I will be like her eventually. Stark, stuck...unable to produce anything tangible.

It's just my theory, but I believe she's under the house, where the porch rests just above the ground. You could remove the lattice that covers the edge and have a look...

I never did get back to work. Barry always made sure that there was a solid reason why I shouldn't whenever the subject came up, and I think I liked that he seemed to need me close.

I suppose he had also needed his high-school sweetheart to stick around when he started college.

Too bad for her that she had planned on going away for school.

She would have been my age by now.

Well, the age of my death.

I suppose even after they find our bodies, me and Becky will always be with him in one way or another.

Molly, when you wake up in the hospital, no matter what the doctors and Barry tell you, don't accept that this is all a dream.

I have more than memories and theories.

I have proof.

Barry doesn't like to throw things away. He has a problem with letting go of the past.

The letters I had found are hidden in the very top part of our closet, inside the old blue gym bag. They are probably still there, right where I left them and just waiting to be read.

And when you have finished, maybe, just maybe you will believe me.

And maybe it will save your life.

I hear the ambulance coming now and I must apologize while I have the chance. I really didn't mean for you to take such a tumble.

Remembering how I had been clinging to consciousness on that hot day gave me the idea.

My hope was only to try to replicate in some way how I first saw that shimmering outline of Becky's form.

Who would have thought that your reaction would be so severe?

The Interview

"We all know what happened to Dr. Doolittle in the end," David muttered to himself. It was how he planned to start the interview when the journalist arrived and got comfortable. He had been repeating it all afternoon in preparation for their conversation as he went in circles, tidying the place up. He was too nervous not to.

There was no use in trying to hide that he had participated in the war on some level. Otherwise, he wouldn't have found himself living in this tenement with his assets frozen. Everyone that took part in the war, no matter the side they chose, had been treated the same. It had been the only way to appease the animals, apart from turning over the doctor.

It seemed that no matter how much David cleaned and reorganized, to him the few rooms in his apartment felt dismal. Despite his best efforts to make the place seem cheerier and inviting for his guest, today wasn't much different. Since losing his wife and most of his belongings, David found it impossible to replicate the charming environment she had established in their previous home.

The memories of things he had lost made his chest tighten. He lowered his head and breathed in deeply, then released the breath as he tilted it back up to cast his gaze around the space one more time, double-checking to verify that he had removed every sign of George's presence. Given her occupation, David was certain that the journalist would be observant.

Once he was convinced that he hadn't missed anything, he allowed his eyes to hover on the small white vase he had set on the table, admiring how the delicate-looking clusters of red and pink flowers spilled out around the edges.

Astilbe had always been his wife's favorite, and he had fiddled with each feather-shaped branch until the thick green stems were positioned at the bottom just right to create the airy arrangement. It was certainly the most attractive thing in his home at the moment.

He was so engrossed in his creation that even though he had been expecting the visitor, he jumped at the soft knocking that sounded just a few steps away. When he swiveled toward the door, he hesitated as he reached for the handle. He wasn't very good at hiding things from people; before the revolt he had never needed to be.

Although he was worried that he could be putting his companion in danger, David cleared his throat then pulled his door open. George had insisted on this meeting, after all, and he knew what was best for him.

The journalist's hand was raised and loosely clenched with her knuckles turned toward him, as if she had been poised to rap on his door again. The sweet scent of fruity-smelling gum wafted toward him as she opened her mouth to speak, but David quickly ushered her inside.

He didn't want to take the chance of someone overhearing them, and he was relieved to see that Joan was not dressed formally, opting to show up in a casual outfit and recreational sneakers. She could be any ordinary visitor, which meant she wouldn't stick out in his neighbors' memories if things didn't go as planned.

They had only spoken over the phone previously, but David thought that she looked pretty much as he had imagined, albeit a bit younger. She was a few inches taller than him, solid yet slim.

He bolted the door and spun toward her. "I hope the lock doesn't startle you."

When his eyes met hers, he added, "It's just, these are strange times."

He tried to look apologetic, although the journalist didn't seem alarmed by his behavior. In fact, as her lips curved upward in a crooked smile. He thought she looked rather amused.

"It's no problem, David."

He gave a quick nod then added, "It is nice to meet you in person, Mrs. Rivers."

Her grin spread as she extended her hand toward him. "It's Miss, but you can call me Joan."

He offered her a weak smile in return as he accepted her hand, giving it a loose shake. "Why don't you come have a seat in the living room, unless you would prefer the dining area?"

David's shoulders stiffened as she rose on her toes to see over him, as if to scan the interior of the next room.

He watched her face closely as she took in the sight of the torn, mismatched furniture, but her enthusiasm didn't seem to waver as she dropped back onto the soles of her feet.

"The living room will be fine."

David tried to release the tension and get his muscles to relax as he waved his hand out toward the room. "You can take whatever seat you would like."

She moved past him to settle into the center of the overstuffed loveseat with her back to the short hallway that led to the washroom and an adjacent bedroom where George was nestled. Thinking it would draw her to the very spot she occupied now, he had purposefully placed a small rectangular coffee table between the seats.

Seeing that his plan had worked caused a nervous rush of energy to sweep through him, and he quickly slid into the old wooden rocker directly across from her before his newly tingling limbs could cause him to sway unnaturally.

As he settled in, she placed a good-sized handbag onto the tabletop, then proceeded to reach inside and pull out a square recording device.

"Do you mind if I use this?"

He coughed dryly as she held it out for him to inspect. Then he tugged at his collar as he spoke. "I would prefer that you took notes in a different manner, if you could."

Her eyes seemed to twinkle as she slipped the recorder back into her bag and began rummaging through its other contents. When she found what she was searching for, she sat back in her seat, clutching a pen and a small notebook.

"Sorry for the trouble," he offered.

"No trouble." Her eyes widened as she went on. "I can see the headline now; another man talks to the animals."

He put his hand on his hip, causing the chair to tilt backward, and offered her a thin smile. "I heard you were tenacious."

She gave a quick nod, her own expression never wavering. "You have to be, in this business, if you ever want to get anywhere."

"I suppose you do." Then he shifted his weight backward and allowed the chair to rock as he continued. "It's actually why I contacted you, specifically."

Her eyes seemed to dull, and a serious look settled over her face as she leaned forward, addressing him in a softer tone. "Is it?"

She cocked her head to the side, seeming to be evaluating him for the first time since her arrival. When her eyes locked onto his, she spoke again, "Before we start, I just want to say: off the record, I can understand a bit of paranoia on your part. But I assure you, there is no reason to be nervous. Just be truthful with your answers, and we will see to it that everything will work out the way it should."

His grin fell, and he wondered if he was really being that obvious. He stopped rocking and planted his feet firmly on the floor in front of the chair, then attempted to change the subject.

"I think I would prefer it if we just got to the questions."

She gave a nod of understanding and sat back. "David, on the record, why are we meeting today?"

"Well, Joan, it's because I have found that I can understand the animals, and they can understand me."

"Like Dr. Doolittle?"

"We all know what happened to Dr. Doolittle in the end, and that's precisely why I requested to take part in this interview, Miss Rivers."

Joan set her pen on top of her notebook and looked up at him. "I hope you don't mind me asking, and this is off the record, but why not keep it a secret?"

He rubbed at the back of his neck. "No offence, of course, but I think that's ill-advised. It would come to light eventually. One way or another."

He lowered his hand and averted his eyes to the floor. "I think the best way to go about it is not to hide, but rather to get people talking as much as possible so that the animals know right out that my intention is not to subject them to the sort of treatment the doctor had over the last decade. I believe that the animals will accept me."

"Maybe." The word came out low, almost in a whisper, and David felt his face flush.

"Why wouldn't they? I'm not here to exploit them or shoot for financial gain as he did. I am just trying to be honest."

She looked down at her notebook and scribbled something hurriedly. When she looked back up, she said, "I agree, that man had no conscience."

David noticed that the pink tinge of her cheeks was becoming brighter as she spoke. "But the doctor started out helping the animals, too, at least until he stopped working alone."

"I don't like what you are insinuating. Even if someone tried to coerce me into it, I don't have the skillset that he did. I wouldn't be able to fulfill government or private contracts in the way he was able."

She clicked her tongue. "The government never expected Dr. Doolittle to take things as far as he did."

David couldn't keep the surprised look from forming on his face, and his voice cracked as he retorted, "So you think the blame should be placed on the private companies then?"

"I don't believe anything is that simple anymore. Not since the animals revolted and proved that they could pull off advanced formulated attacks against us."

David's hand migrated toward one of the small holes in the cushion that padded the rocking chair, and he began pulling at the stuffing as he replied indignantly, "Those attacks were just warnings."

"If you say so." The words slipped out low between her clenched teeth, as if she hadn't meant to speak them aloud at all. When she picked her pen back up and raised her eyes to him, she continued in her normal tone. "Well, let's move on by learning how you came about having this talent."

His fingers paused mid pull as he looked up at her and furrowed his brow. "What do you mean?"

"Dr. Doolittle claimed that he had always had this ability, but when his past was investigated, they determined that the telepathic phenomena regarding animals started after he was hospitalized from a severe blow to the head."

David crinkled his nose. "Nothing like that."

She raised her eyebrows at him as if surprised. "No?"

"I simply woke up one day and could hear them. It was as if a translator had been turned on in my brain."

"No injuries from the war then?" She blew a big bubble and popped it with her teeth.

He had forgotten about the aroma he had noticed at the door, and he wondered if chewing gum was a nervous habit. The idea brought attention to his own actions, and he pulled his hand away from the stuffing, opting to clutch the armrest instead.

"Other than my pride, no."

She tapped her pen against the paper impatiently and popped another smaller bubble between her teeth. "Can I ask why you decided to call my number? I mean, besides that fact that you heard I was tenacious."

"I was advised to handle the matter this way."

"By your wife?"

The question flustered him further, and he spat out his answer rapidly. "My wife got maimed beyond help in one of the events. Some poor, confused creatures couldn't tell what side she was on after the military got involved."

Joan fired back, "Then who?"

"My dog, George." The words left his mouth before he could stop them, but to his surprise, Joan seemed unfazed by his announcement.

"And where is George now?"

"He came back right after the original uprising ended."

Her voice remained even as she responded. "You should have reported that."

"But he is my dog." David shifted uncomfortably in his seat; he had said too much, but there was no going back now.

An amused smirk made its way on to her face as she asked, "Is he? Or are you his human?"

David's lips twitched. "What are you going to do?"

"That depends. Where is George now?"

His stomach flopped, and he leaned forward, folding his arms around it. "I gave him my bed after he returned from the war. He was injured. He is all I have left."

She jotted a few words down then asked, "What side was he on, and what breed is he?"

His words came out in shaky sudden burst. "Dammit. It doesn't matter what side he was on. He is family. As for breed, who can say...a random mixed dog?"

Her eyebrows arched as she peeked up from her notes. "A mutt? How big?"

"He doesn't appreciate being called a mutt," David growled.

She closed the notebook as she offered an apology. "I am sorry, David. It is illegal to harbor a fugitive former pet. So, are you harboring a fugitive here?"

"He told me to ask for you."

"I understand that, but it's procedure. I need to ask you if you are a spy for the animals, David?"

"Are you a spy for the humans?" he retorted, wondering if she had been expertly steering the conversation all along.

"I am no spy, David."

"Humans have had the upper hand for too long," he shouted as he bounced up from his seat.

Joan reached for her purse and shoved the notebook and pen inside as David continued. "Don't you try anything, Joan. At this point, running for the door would be foolhardy, and I guarantee whatever you have in that purse can't save you from both of us. George is right in the other room, and he has keen ears. He will protect me from you."

"You misunderstand, David."

"How so?"

"George got you to initiate this interview because he is having you put down."

As if called to attention, his tricolored friend appeared in the hallway. His tail and his ears were raised to attention.

David took a step back as the dog made eye contact then crouched forward with his hackles raised in warning.

"George?" David questioned.

Joan responded, "You yourself said it, David. We all know what happened to Dr. Doolittle in the end, and we can't take a chance of it ever happening again."

David's mouth hung open as George addressed him. "It's for your own good, David. I know what's best for you."

"But George." He paused, licking his dry lips before continuing, "I called the journalist, like you..." he was unable to get the rest of his words out.

Joan let out a snicker then addressed the dog. "That was a good one, George. I almost wish I could have a chat with you myself."

George took a few steps forward, and David took another step away, bumping into the wall with his back.

"Now, David, don't give the nice lady any trouble," George scolded.

Joan and George's words stung. David felt hot tears prickle at the corners of his eyes as he lowered himself to the floor, astonished by the turn of events.

Once he was hunkered down, dread awakened within him, and a coldness seemed to spread throughout his body. He had been betrayed. David reached up with one hand clasping at his throat as the shock took complete control.

He watched silently as George move forward again, stopping between him and Joan. "You were always a good human, David. Let's keep it that way."

Then George sat on his haunches, facing him with his ears bent back, and David's eyes flitted from his companion over to Joan.

He stared at her, still perplexed, as she pulled a large syringe from her handbag and stood. Her words came out in a robotic fashion as she approached, addressing him. "As part of the treaty, an undisclosed agreement was made by the government. I just had to confirm the facts from you before I initialized your termination."

David was too disoriented to respond, and he sat numbly by as Joan slid a little white cap off the end of the needle then pointed it at him menacingly.

"George, you understand that his body will be confiscated for study?"

The dog let out a single bark toward Joan then addressed David. "At least I know you will always continue to do good." George stood and turned so that his back was facing David before he spoke again. "Rest easy, old friend."

The Other Side of the Door

William heard the familiar tap-tapping of Cynthia's knuckles as they rapped on his door. She always did it in such a gentle way, so as not to wake him if he was in bed. He grinned from ear to ear but remained still, knowing in his absence she would slip a note under the door, and although he was excited to see what she had written, he hesitated. It had been a long night, a rough shift, and she would be just heading in to work herself.

He certainly didn't want to hold her up.

When they did talk, they often lost track of time, him sitting on the cold linoleum tile by his closed door and her no doubt kneeling on the thinly carpeted hallway rug, even though it was stained and worn from overuse and infrequent care.

She lived only a few flights above him, yet even before the outbreak, it was rare for them to see each other face-to-face. Their schedules in general made it nearly impossible for them to meet. He worked through the night, and her shift always started with the dawn. They had only been on one real date in the past year. That had been right before the virus had taken hold of the world. Since then they had decided to remain in touch as pen pals rather than take the chance of infecting one another by close proximity.

Even separated as they were, her fondness for him was evident with each note she passed beneath the door, and he admittedly cherished every single citrus-scented page. Thoughts of her made his stomach feel queasy. He longed to see her again without the barrier that separated them, yet he didn't dare.

The loneliness had been wearing on her as well, he knew. Not for the first time, she had breached the subject of her restless heart in the latest letter, suggesting that they throw caution to the wind. He hoped that his response had eased her sadness and set her back into the right state of mind, promising that he would still care for her when a vaccine was released.

He wondered how long ago that had been as he picked at the dry, cracked skin on his hands and tried to think back. The only distinctive part of that day he recalled was being disheartened at the sight of the last sheet of sky-blue stationery that she had come to expect as he tore it from his notepad.

Now just one other color remained of the original spring-themed trio, and it was a bright green. He didn't quite care for the shade, but it would have to do if he felt the need to respond to her message.

"Of course, I will," he quipped, once again grinning as he dropped his hands and shifted his gaze to the ceiling. Writing a letter would help break up the monotony of the passing days.

He had lost the yearning to leave the building for recreation some time ago after a careless man bumped into him on the sidewalk. Cynthia and his weekly grocery deliveries had been his only reprieve ever since his office instructed him to remain at home. He never argued with the decision; there was no real reason that he couldn't continue his technical support job from here.

He furrowed his brows thoughtfully and shook his head. The latter didn't really count, since the delivery person dropped the bags by his door and almost always left before he could thank them. He let out a sigh. It was for the best anyway, he knew.

The sound of the neighbor's door slamming jolted him upright. The walls between his unit and theirs seemed paper-thin at times. He wished his neighbor could show him the same courtesy that Cynthia did, but truth be told, he seemed jealous of the relationship. He often banged pots and pans or turned the radio up during their chats in the hallway.

William rubbed at the back of his neck sleepily and wondered whether she had made sure to shove the note all the way through the gap. The idea of that four-by-six-inch rectangular letter falling into his neighbor's hands teased him and drove him out of bed.

When he entered the room to collect it, he breathed deeply. The familiar scent of her perfume seemed to fill every corner. His smile faltered as he reached down to retrieve the light purple page that was her usual stationery.

The imprinted sun that generally smiled at him from the upper right corner instead held a drawn-on frown. His stomach turned. The note was printed in thick black marker, which was not her usual form either. Generally, her letters held flowing cursive that danced across the page in such a way that he could scarcely stop himself from humming a tune as he read.

This note was something else entirely, more of a notice than anything. Those ugly thick lines formed only three offensive words.

His mind spun as he realized the very note itself could be contaminated. He dropped it onto the tiled floor in disgust as he ran to the kitchen to wash his hands.

When he was satisfied with the raw, red look of his fingers and palms, he turned the steaming faucet off before opening the cupboard where he kept his cleaning supplies. After donning a pair of rubber gloves, he retrieved the bottle of spray disinfectant and a small garbage bag from the upper shelf.

Using half of the liquid contents of the bottle as his weapon, he attacked the tainted note on the floor where it had landed. But the more he sprayed, the more Cynthia's perfume seemed to surround him, taunting him.

Taking a deep breath and holding it, he bent to retrieve the smudged page and place it within the thick plastic bag, which he then tied tight.

Planning to carry it into the hall and drop it into the garbage chute, he reached for the handle of his door and hesitated, his fingers outstretched and hovering. He pulled his gloved hand away and stepped back. Tears prickled at the corners of his eyes, threatening to escape.

He had no way of knowing if she had taken the proper precautions before she made her way to his door. No way of knowing if she had infected the entire corridor. He spun on his heels and headed toward the kitchen with the bag still clutched in his hand.

Working as quickly as possible, he set the bag inside the sink and removed his gloves, intent on dropping them into the basin as well. His hands shook as he rewashed them before moving to engage the sink plug.

They were still shaking as he reached up into the cupboard, causing him to knock the lemony wood polish and all-purpose cleaner out onto the counter. To his dismay, a jug of floor cleaner soon followed. This one didn't stop at the countertop as the first two had. It continued moving until it rolled off the edge and onto the floor, hitting in such a way that the bottom of the container cracked, allowing orange liquid to seep out.

He gulped at the sight but continued searching for the bleach as he recited, "First things first, first things first, first things first." His heart battered against his chest.

Once the bleach was in hand, he removed its cap and poured the entire bottle into the sink, effectively covering its contents. With that done, he took a deep breath and reached for his mop to clean up the spilled liquid.

Try as he might, as he worked, he couldn't shake thoughts of Cynthia from filling his mind, and after he finished the task, he began pacing the floor with his phone in hand and muttering her name while he flipped through the contacts.

Cynthia had given him her phone number before they went on their first date, but he hadn't had a need to use it. She always seemed to stop by with a note whenever she was on his mind.

He chose her name from the list and hit send.

There was an almost immediate sharp tone in his ear, followed by a robotic voice that said, "This number is not in service. If you would like to make a call, please hang up and try again."

He ended the call and repeated it. Once more, the automated message played in his ear. His chest felt tight, and he gasped for breath. Dropping his phone as he moved, he rushed back into the kitchen and stood over the sink, his hands gripping the edge as he began taking slow, controlled breaths.

Where most of the units had at least one window, his did not. Instead, the previous tenant had hung curtains around a small mirror and nailed it in above the faucet to represent one. He had never bothered to remove it.

Glancing up into his reflection, he barely recognized the person that stared back at him. The hair was flat as a pancake on one side of his head and spiked out at odd angles on the other. His bloodshot eyes were rimmed with dark circles and appeared sunk in against his otherwise pale face.

He tried to focus on taking slow, steady breaths as he closed his eyes and allowed his head to hang forward. It hardly mattered what he looked like now that Cynthia had betrayed him anyway.

A gurgling below him broke his concentration, and he opened his eyes to inspect the contents of the sink basin.

Considering his haste to fill the sink, he wasn't surprised to see that the rubber gloves had floated up to the surface. He knew that a small amount of air must have been trapped within the fingers and that the bleach should have destroyed any microscopic germs that had come into contact with them, yet he couldn't seem to tear his eyes away.

He relaxed his grip and leaned in closer, breathing in the strong aroma of the chemical. Little brown flecks of something seemed to speckle the rubber, and they appeared to be twitching ever so slightly.

The sight caused him to bend forward and lean in even further. His brow crinkled as he squinted, trying to focus on the organisms. He caught sight of one of the specks as it moved from the wrist to the finger on one glove, then another as it darted from the finger to the mid-hand area. He cocked his head to the side as he stared and contemplated what he was seeing.

After several minutes, his eyes began to feel dry and uncomfortable from the strain, causing him to lean back away. They stung in response as he blinked rapidly in an attempt to replenish their moisture. When the stinging subsided, he repositioned himself to peer back into the basin.

Now it seemed all the specks had begun to move, darting back and forth along their hand-shaped raft, as if looking for an escape. He tried to track their movements, but there were too many of the organisms.

The hair on his right arm bristled with a strange sensation, and he jerked backward, away from the sink. As he stumbled to the floor, the sensation moved up his arm, as though something was crawling on his skin. His eyes grew wide with the realization.

Hoping to trap the culprit beneath his palm and get a better look, he shifted onto his knees and raised his left hand, preparing to bring it down hard. When the sensation reached just below his elbow on the offending arm, he struck. Keeping his hand firmly in place, he trained his eyes on the spot and slowly lifted it.

His mouth gaped at the sight. Several of the brown flecks made frenzied movements beneath his palm. They had escaped the sink. Before he could react further, they leapt forward, flinging themselves toward his face. He fought the urge to scream and clapped his mouth shut, his teeth knocking together painfully.

Deep down he knew it was too late, even before he felt the tickling sensation erupt in his mouth and move to his throat. Resigned to his fate, he crossed his arms over his chest, hugging himself in a tight embrace, and began rocking back and forth.

A gentle tap-tapping noise sounded from the other side of the door, but William remained in his spot on the floor, wishing Cynthia had never existed.

II

Tales from Sumir

Cultivating Wrath

Jaali stared straight ahead at the misshapen tree, his fists clenched so tightly, he could feel his nails burrowing into his flesh. His cheeks burned, and he knew if his guardian, Aaminah, looked at him she would see bright orange flames lit in the pupils of his eyes. But she was focused on the story she needed to tell. Her voice was steady as she began.

"In the beginning, our universe was a vast, empty void. This void, it is said, contained space for endless worlds to fit inside."

He clenched his jaw and willed his heart to slow. It was a story he knew already, could recite by heart, so why did Aaminah think it would help soothe them? Other younglings sat cross-legged around the ancient tree. They seemed to be listening, to understand what she was telling them, as if it explained the reason for their sudden departure.

"One day out of the void emerged two powerful celestial beings, Eaki and Aya." Her ominous tone penetrated his thoughts.

"They had traveled from another universe far away in search of a place where there was room for their godlike children to grow.

"They brought with them the knowledge of creation and set about molding a simple world to live together in the center of the universe."

Each time she paused in her speech, Jaali's stomach turned. How could he just sit here? He was, after all, partially to blame; all the younglings were. They had known the man wasn't kin, and still they went to him. They could smell it on him, his strange magic, from the moment he stepped out of the shadows of the huts and into the trail that led from their village. Still, they proceeded toward him, curious at his sudden appearance. They should have realized he was one of the arcane wizards. At the very least, they should have heeded Erol's words as the guardian called to them to stop advancing on the stranger.

"One by one, as their children were born, Eaki and Aya raised them to adolescence." She paused, and Jaali looked up as Aaminah placed her hand on a whimpering youngling's head to comfort her. "Knowing at this age their children would begin to become restless and crave a deeper purpose, they sent them out into this universe to create a single world of their own to cultivate and control. They were each given a limited number of enchanted supplies to use. This is how our sun, our moons, and each unique planet came into existence." She hesitated as she made her way back toward the center of the group of children where the ancient tree stood.

Swift decisions had been made. They had all been moved to this place, this town away from everything they knew. The runes engraved into the tree's craggy branches still glowed a bright yellow with the magic of the jinns' travel from the plane of the emerald mountains, their home. A land where magic seemed to emanate from the very air.

Thrust into this unfamiliar land. This place where magic didn't hum all around but only throbbed dully from the tree.

Aaminah reached out and placed a hand on the tree's bark as if she could hear what Jaali was thinking. "So it went until Aya gave birth to triplet daughters. Sophia, the first-born, Akila, the middle daughter, and Mia, the youngest. The two younger siblings bickered constantly and fought for their parents' attention. As the girls neared adolescence, their competitive nature only grew worse." Her voice cracked, and Jaali looked up at her as she continued. Her face appeared calm; her eyes moved slowly over each child.

"Sophia overheard Eaki and Aya discussing her two younger sisters and was troubled to hear that they doubted the girls would be able to sustain their creations for long."

They had been taught this myth since birth, taken to the ancient caves, studied the stone tablets, so how could this help anything? Jaali knew how he was supposed to feel, but he couldn't control that, could he?

"When the time came, Eaki gave them each a chunk of enchanted clay, seeds, and some drops of his celestial blood. He then sent them into the universe to create their individual worlds.

"Sophia followed her sisters, and after watching them bicker and fight, decided that they could not be trusted to fulfill their father's wishes."

Aaminah took a deep breath and exhaled. Jaali swore he could feel the release of her breath on his hot cheeks, cooling them.

"Determined to help them succeed and make her father proud, she persuaded them to combine the resources to create one larger, more diverse world together so they could share equally in the responsibilities."

Jaali shifted uncomfortably in the damp grass. Most of the jinn had panicked and fled. A few had stayed as protectors of the emerald mountains. Why couldn't he stay? He was rushed away so fast, he hadn't even had time to fully grasp what had happened.

Aaminah raised her voice. "Akila and Mia eagerly handed over the halves of their clay that was meant to be the base for their three small worlds. Sophia lumped the pieces of clay together and carefully started to shape the world. As she worked, the younger sisters teased and tormented one another."

Jaali swallowed, gulping air as his chest tightened into a knot, like a cramp.

"Sophia borrowed inspiration for many of her designs in this new world from stories her parents had told her of their favorite planet in the distant universe they had come from." Aaminah clapped her hands, drawing attention back to her story. Jaali crossed his arms in front of him, his hands still balled into fists.

"She created a flat mass of land and surrounded it with water. She molded rivers, mountains, and valleys. When everything seemed to be balanced, she shook the remaining tiny flecks of clay from her hands, creating small chunks of light in orbit around the world."

Travel to the human plane was supposed to be reserved as a rite of passage for those who wanted it bad enough to earn it, not those running in fright. He slammed his fist into the dirt. Jaali wanted to fight back, to prepare, not to hide out.

Again, Aaminah's voice rose. "Satisfied that she had included everything required for obtaining harmony, she went to work molding a race of humans. Sophia carefully considered every little detail before applying the final touches and bringing them to life. To her, free will was the only real gift they needed to thrive.

"Sophia was content with the intelligent beings that she created and enjoyed watching them learn and progress."

Jaali tried to remember the stone tablets and what they taught. He attempted to swallow back the guilt and rage. Instead, he could only think of poor Erol, the adolescent that had been watching them at the time of the attack. The jinn should be after the monster that attacked them. Instead, they punish one of their own and run!

A few of the younglings murmured something Jaali couldn't make out. Aaminah clapped again, drawing his attention and gaze back to her.

"Mia and Akila also watched the humans. Although the people were quite intelligent, they appeared weak to Mia and Akila. The sisters decided they would each make a magical race and have a contest between them to determine who of the two could create the most powerful beings.

"Akila created the elemental spirits, the jinn, born of smokeless fire.

"In response, Mia created beings with great arcane magic and taught them to hate the jinn and to pursue them relentlessly."

Jaali spat on the ground at the mention of the arcane wizards. He couldn't stop the rage. He was angry, and it flowed through him like lava pushing for a way out. Jaali looked at the ground, ashamed. Was he the only one that was mad? He wanted to seek and destroy, not run and hide. Why should they be ripped from all they knew?

Aaminah was wandering in his direction now. He tried to focus on her slow movements.

"As the two races fought one another, Sophia's race of humans was often caught in the middle. Not having natural magic themselves, they were unable to put up an adequate defense."

She looked right at him then as she continued, and he shifted his gaze to the tree.

"Sophia couldn't bear to see her humans so abused. She jumped down onto the plate of land, splitting in into several pieces and spreading them apart across the vast seas that she had created. Hoping to spare her human race from future devastation, she placed them all onto one of the masses of land."

Aaminah cleared her throat loudly from beside him, and he jerked his gaze from the tree to her.

"Akila and Mia continued to pit their creations against one another, but it became apparent that the two species were somewhat equally matched.

"Still, craving victory, Akila used the last of her clay to create beings of pure light and energy.

"In response, Mia created demons of pure darkness, able to harness shadows and live on pure fear. Again, the sisters sent their creations on a path of destruction."

Aaminah looked into Jaali's eyes as she spoke. How could she so willingly accept this fate?

"By this time, all being intelligent and curious species, they had discovered various ways to travel the great seas. Once again, the humans were thrust into a war they had no chance of surviving. Sophia scolded her sisters for being so careless as she watched her creation brought to the brink of extinction."

Jaali watched her as she moved away and bent to wipe the tears from one of the youngling's eyes before speaking again.

"Still, the sisters ignored Sophia's pleas to stop their vicious campaign. The battles raged on until only a few humans remained. Sophia's anger grew, and she was filled with rage at the destruction of the creations she had worked so hard on." Aaminah stood, and her gaze again returned to Jaali, sending a shiver through him.

Her voice boomed louder still, words spilled from her mouth in a frenzy, and she flailed her arms. "Sophia ripped and shredded the very fabric of the world, tearing each species away from the other and separating them into five different planes, with the humans in the center-most realm. Once these changes were made, Sophia knew they could not be undone."

Jaali swore he saw a flash of red and orange deep in her pupils as her gaze shifted from him back to the others.

"Still disgusted with her sisters, she created two more planes; the realm of the goddess was set above all the rest. She forbade her sisters from joining her there. In the seventh plane, she threw her remaining ingredients in at random. Sophia then ordered her sisters to live in that realm of chaos far below the other planes." A groan escaped her lips; Jaali could see beads of perspiration on her brow. She weaved her way around the youngsters, her movements now jerky.

"Only then did her younger siblings stop bickering amongst themselves. Seeing what had befallen their world, the two younger sisters felt guilty and longed to earn Sophia's favor back."

Aaminah turned in a circle and lowered her voice. "Akila and Mia still had a few supplies remaining. Seven drops of creator's blood and seven seeds from the sacred tree." She gestured toward the large tree as she went on.

"Akila took the tree seeds and put them in each new plane that had been created, connecting them once again in secret locations that would allow passage from plane to plane."

Jaali looked at the tree again; the runes were now nothing more than dark scorch marks embedded in its gray bark.

"Mia created seven powerful gems to represent each of the planes and offered the stones to Sophia as penance.

"Sophia had missed her sisters and was impressed with their gifts. She allowed them to remain with her in the realm of the goddess to help watch over the original five planes."

A few of the younglings whispered. Aaminah clapped her hands a third time, indicating her story was not yet over.

"As time went on, the creatures below in the seventh realm were all but forgotten. Left unchecked to mature and evolve on their own without the guidance of the goddesses, they became loathsome and villainous."

Somewhere nearby, a jinni released a loud gasp. "Shhh." Aaminah put her finger to her lips.

"Some of the creatures blamed the humans' existence on the separation of the planes and were deeply resentful. Others missed them, especially the jinn, and passed the knowledge of what had happened down through the generations."

Aaminah bent down over him; Jaali could feel her warm breath against his ear as she whispered sweetly, her voice like a song. "We will get them both back, one way or another."

As she stood again, Jaali unclenched his fists and moved to his feet. Aaminah reached her arms around him. Jaali hugged her back and let the tears roll down his face as she finished her story.

"Most humans forgot about magic altogether. This is why we chose to come here. We will build a new life in the safety of this ancient sapling."

Jaali buried his wrath deep inside; it was only a matter of time until the arcane sorcerer found their new village. A time to fight back would come. He would be ready, and he would make the arcane wizard suffer.

Bavmordia Part One ~ The Journey

Bavmorda's bones creaked as she stood and stretched. With her piercing blue eyes, smooth skin, and long, thin nose, she was not at all what she appeared to be. Centuries old, she was ancient even for a member of the arcane species, and she refused to share the secret of her youthful appearance with anyone. She glanced down at the boulder she had been using as a chair, and a yawn escaped her mouth.

She was incurably bored and had been for what felt to her like ages. In her mind, her life had peaked while she was still a juvenile, when all the races had still roamed Sumir together.

She walked slowly across the glen until her feet hit the edge of the stone pathway. She had laid it herself long ago to help her from slipping when she made her way up the gently sloped concave side of the valley that led toward her secluded cottage.

Bav had seen the separation of the realms as both a blessing and a curse.

She had always been a bit different from her arcane brothers and sisters. Instead of hunting jinn, as she was supposed to, as a youth she had been drawn to the humans. In her inexperienced eyes, most of them seemed corrupt, and she had become preoccupied with using her magical abilities on them in fantastical ways. While frequent battles raged between magical races, barely anyone had taken notice of her growing obsession.

When the barrier first formed, splitting the magical races from one another, she had lived in the makeshift settlements that sprouted up, and for a while, she even felt at home. Without access to the jinn, many of her arcane comrades grew curious about the nonmagical beings that had caused their world to be turned upside down. At first, Bav had been happy to join in the discussions. But as time passed, so did their interest in what she had to say.

As Bav neared the top, the heavy air seemed to hum with electricity. The hair on her arms and neck prickled. She looked up into the sky, but there was no sign of an impending storm in the fluffy white clouds that hung against the pale blue backdrop.

Straight ahead, the world began to waver, rippling outward like water in a disturbed pond. Bav strode closer without hesitation. She was too old and had seen far too much to be afraid.

The moment she pushed through the veil and stepped out onto the other side, she knew there was only one place she could be. The ground beneath her feet felt hard and cold. On three sides she was surrounded by metal transport devices, and in front of her was the long brick façade of a building. She stood in awe for a moment, taking in her new environment, unconcerned with how or why she had gained access to the human realm. Her heart pounded with excitement.

A shrill bell sounded from the building in front of her, and the voices inside rose a notch.

Within moments, dozens of human figures pushed their way out the doors and headed in her direction. Many trotted quickly past her without so much as a sideways glance. They crowded into the transports and exited the lot.

When the stream of humans began to trickle down, Bav's eyes again darted around the parking lot. Across from her, a woman stood beside the open door to a white car. As their eyes met, the woman smiled at Bav and called to her, "Do you want a ride to lunch?" The woman looked down at the jewelry on her wrist. "Come on. There is room in my car."

Bav nodded and walked toward the vehicle as the woman slid into her seat and shut the door. She approached the car and tested the door handle with her fingers, mirroring what she had seen the humans do. She took a quick step back as the door popped open before sliding herself onto the seat.

The woman turned to her and offered her hand. "I'm Rachel. Is it your first day?"

"Yes." She gave Rachel's hand a fast, loose shake, "Bav."

"We don't have very long. We better get moving."

Bav studied Rachel as she moved the vehicle down the path and out onto the road. Steering the machine didn't look that hard, and she would have magic to help her...she just needed to persuade Rachel to give it to her.

"I bet you're substituting for Carl, aren't you? That explains why I didn't see you in the halls. His classes are clear on the other side of the school from mine."

Smiling politely back at Rachel, Bav grasped at her necklace and stroked the enchanted opal that hung from the chain.

"Oh, you probably don't want to talk about work. Sorry, I am rambling. Teaching can be taxing some days."

As the car came to a stop outside of a building with a neon sign that said *DELI*, Bav wrapped her fingers more tightly around the opal and turned to Rachel. "Rachel, why don't you go in without me."

Ignoring Bav, Rachel let out a groan of annoyance and slid down lower in her seat, shielding her eyes. "One of my colleagues is here." She let out a huff. "That one goes out of his way to unnerve me, I swear. We don't have time to go somewhere else. I can't wait for them to put a hot lunch cafeteria in the building; the plans are in the works. I do hate getting lunch alone. I even keep some fruit in the back... I am rambling again." Rachel turned toward her and sat up. "Sorry, what did you say?"

Bav needed a moment to breathe before she started her search for the perfect pupil. Rachel certainly wouldn't do at all. "Go inside and meet your friend there for lunch. He can give you a ride back to work. What did you say his name was again?"

"Bill, but that seems..."

Bav shook her head and rubbed the opal harder. "Rachel, get out of my car and go talk to him." This time her pupils seemed to pulsate in unison with Bav's words, and her eyes took on a cloudy appearance.

"You are right, Bav. I am glad we met, but I should go."

"And Rachel, forget I was here." Rachel nodded back and jumped from the car, racing into the deli. Bav shook her head and released her talisman, whispering to herself, "I must be out of practice." She turned to open the passenger door and walked around the back of the car, eyeing the black briefcase that rested on the back seat next to three very ripe bananas. Curious about the contents, she pulled the back door open and leaned in.

Several minutes passed as she fumbled with the latches, and in her excitement at finally getting them to release she allowed the contents to spill out onto the seat. Amidst the papers was a small white box with a large red cross on the cover. A peek inside was all she needed to verify that it was a kit for simple first aid.

The bland contents of the vehicle helped to fortify her belief that Rachel was not the kind of person she was looking for. Using powerful magic on someone as innocent as she seemed would take the fun out of it.

With her curiosity satisfied, she made her way into the driver's seat and stared at the dashboard.

She had been studying Rachel as she maneuvered the maze of streets. Although she was unsure of what all the symbols meant, she had noted that one of the floor pedals seemed to make the car move faster while the other pedal had seemed to slow it down. She tapped the controls at her feet lightly as she watched the gages adjust.

Confident that she had a handle on it, she shifted the car from P to D with her foot firmly in position. As she pulled away from the curb, leaving the deli behind, she whispered a spell for guidance away from the bustling area. The car almost seemed to take on a mind of its own as it moved along the busy roads.

Nothing she saw much surprised her. She had, after all, witnessed first-hand the drastic changes that her own realm had gone through over the centuries.

It was true that the human realm seemed to have advanced more technologically, but then there had always been whispers that time passed differently in each of the realms. And of course, humans, being nonmagical, would have been pushed to find other more creative ways to advance their world and solve problems that for the arcane would have easily been taken care of with magic.

When the car came to a quieter neighborhood, Bav directed it to stop. She was eager to begin her search, but she also wanted to explore the area a bit more thoroughly without interruption. She clutched at her gemstone, willing it to help keep her unnoticed amidst the locals before she began to wander the nearby streets.

With her magical abilities, it hadn't been at all hard for her to procure a vehicle and come up with a technique to drive it.

In the hours that passed, she wandered, practicing using the enhanced power of her opal on the humans.

She approached a woman on a bench and used the persuasive properties of the opal to get her to leave her glasses behind as she stood to go.

Bav smirked as she lifted the wireframe onto her face. The image of the world blurred slightly through the lenses. She whispered a clarifying spell before making her way back to the car, her confidence in her ability to take whatever she wanted from the humans newly reinforced.

Once again in the driver's seat, Bav twisted her hair up onto her head, securing it into a loose bun. She turned her face from side to side, admiring her new look in the mirror.

She was ready; she felt it deep within her old bones.

A look of panic and dread was pasted on the girl's face as she moved steadily down the sidewalk and past Bav's idling car. She had been waiting there, watching the humans from the front seat.

She perked up and rolled down the window to call out to her, sure that the juvenile was running from something. "Hi, there. You look lost. Is everything okay?"

The girl only nodded in response.

Bav's glasses slid down her nose as she signaled the girl with her hands. Each time she pushed the glasses back into position, loose strands of her hair would begin tickling at her face. "Come closer, I won't bite."

The teen took a few hesitant steps toward the car, and Bav again straightened the sliding glasses, causing more hair to fall from her makeshift bun. When she looked back up, a genuine curiosity filled Bav as her eyes locked with the girl's. Odd purple flecks seemed to dominate the teenager's irises, a genetic anomaly of some sort, she was certain. She had never noted such a color in a human's eyes before.

"I'm just on my way home."

She looked the girl up and down as she walked the last few steps toward the car. The girl's eyes swept over the contents in the back seat before returning to Bav's face. She suddenly seemed vacant, as if lost in thought, and Bav cleared her throat to get her attention. She pointed at the girl's ripped sleeve, adding, "You're bleeding."

Bav considered the nervous way the girl had been chewing at her lip; now her cheeks were becoming notably brighter.

She didn't want to miss the opportunity to gain a perfect pupil. She needed more time to figure out what the girl had been up to. The girl turned away, and Bav grabbed at her talisman. "Wait... I have some bandages in my first aid kit."

The girl shook her head. "No, thank you."

Bav gripped the opal harder. She didn't want this one to get away. "Can I drop you off somewhere? I'm headed out of the city myself."

The girl only shuffled her feet in response. Afraid that she would turn and run, Bav frantically rubbed the talisman as she offered up the first thing that popped into her head. "Banana?"

The thought of losing her chance to teach the girl a lesson caused her stomach to turn as she reached into the backseat and grabbed for one of the pieces of fruit. She let out a low sigh of relief as she poked the end out of the open window and the girl reached for it, offering her thanks.

"I have more around here somewhere," she added as she reached behind the seat to grab another. "I'm Bav." She was careful to smile sweetly as she reached back toward the open window.

"No, thank you." The girl smiled back at her. "It's nice to meet you."

Her confidence faltered. The teen had said no.

Bav looked deeply into the girl's eyes. She could see that they were no longer bright and clear. She was under the opal's influence, and yet this juvenile seemed to possess the ability to deny her requests, at least to a small extent.

Bav scolded herself for being so rash; she obviously just hadn't given the talisman long enough to work on the girl. To be sure, she calmly reached for the stone on her necklace again. She held it between her two fingers and rubbed it lightly. "Well, come on, get in. I do have a schedule to keep."

"Thanks." This time, the girl responded in an almost robotic fashion as she opened the door and slid into the leather-covered seat, stowing her backpack on the floor by her feet.

Bav patiently waited to begin her interrogation until the girl had cleaned up her wounded arm. She was pleasantly surprised when the girl started asking her questions, and she quickly took over the questioning, caressing her opal as she attempted to learn more about her.

But the longer she probed the girl, the more she felt like someone or something was probing her right back. She began to tense up from uncertainty. The opal talisman her mother had enchanted for her so many ages ago had never failed her in the past.

A sharp pain shot through her skull, and she involuntarily pressed her foot harder onto the pedal. Something was not right. It felt like some sort of magical attack.

Her skull felt heavy, and her eyes felt strained. She stared over at her passenger, wondering if she could somehow be the culprit. But the girl seemed unfazed, at least until she caught sight of her worried companion from the corner of her eye.

As the girl turned to face her, Bav held her breath, certain she would somehow catch on to her ill intentions as she inspected her now.

She didn't look concerned until her eyes locked onto Bav's feet. The girl then quickly turned away.

At that moment, Bav's vision blurred; someone or something was trying to take over. As another sharp pain reverberated throughout her head, she was pushed back out of the way of whatever was inside her. Panic took hold of her as she realized she had lost the battle to maintain control of herself. She could hear her own voice, but she couldn't make out the muffled words of the conversation with her passenger.

Trapped in her own head, Bav cursed. She had not been prepared and had been open to attack. But what or who could have reached her in the human realm, she couldn't understand.

When control of her body was relinquished back to her, Bav found herself sitting alone in the parked car. She had lost her pupil. But how?

The entire encounter seemed fuzzy now. As if she had been in a dream state the whole time.

Bav looked up into the mirror and shook her head. In her excitement, she had made a mistake. She had acted too hastily and missed the very important fact that the girl had not been entirely human. Couldn't have been. The way that the teen had maintained some semblance of control while under the opal's powers should have told her that.

The next time she would lay low until she was better acquainted with her pupil. She would wait to strike until she was absolutely sure.

On the other hand, she hadn't missed the way the girl had ogled her bare feet.

Bav wiggled her large toes, recalling that none of the humans she had seen so far had seemed to tolerate the feel of the ground beneath them. She supposed it was because so much of the land was paved over. If she hoped to better fit in amongst them, she would have to keep them covered.

Bav didn't want to dwell on the encounter any longer.

Determined not to repeat her past mistakes again, she set back off on her search for someone to teach.

Bavmordia Part Two ~ Lessons

Bav watched her prey with an awkward smile displayed on her face. This was exactly the kind of human she had been looking for. The pretty specimen was undeniably vain, and the way she interacted with the people that flocked around her was callous, often cruel. Bav was going to knock the wind right out of her.

She fidgeted with the opal talisman that hung from her neck as the young human thrust her leg out from beneath the table she was sitting at, causing an unsuspecting passerby to stumble and fall forward onto her hands and knees. Bav covered her mouth with her hand to stifle a giggle as she realized the girl's intentions were not unlike her own.

"Oops," the attacker blurted as her table of admirers bellowed in laughter. "Didn't see you there." When the tormentor pushed herself up from her seat, luxuriant glossy red hair flowed down past her waist. She smoothed down her skirt before swiping a napkin from the tabletop.

Her victim, a young woman that appeared to be about the same age, remained on the ground, cradling her bloodied knee. "You did that on purpose, Tarah." Her eyes locked onto her predator as Tarah made her slow, exaggerated approach.

Bav's glasses slid forward on her face as she eyed her prize greedily from her seat at the next table.

Tarah shrugged and bent down, dropping the napkin beside her victim. "Prove it, Casey."

Bav's smile only grew wider as she witnessed the treachery in front of her.

Tarah righted herself and moved past Casey, and her entourage jumped up from their seats, fumbling with their trays as they scurried after her.

Bav was in no rush to get up; she had been watching Tarah for days and knew her routine. She had wanted to be sure this time. She breathed a sigh of relief and shuffled her uncomfortable feet under the table. Her toes felt trapped inside the large leather boots she had adopted since she had tried to pick up her last pupil.

A yawn escaped her mouth as she finally rose to make her way to where her parked car waited. She had plenty of time to rest up and allow her feet room to breathe before she would meet with Tarah.

A nap would renew her energy, and she needed a lot of it if she was going to go through with the girl's lesson.

The sun was setting low when she pulled up along the curb outside of Tarah's house. The smile melted off her face when she glanced at the passenger seat; her excitement was momentarily forgotten. She stretched forward, reaching for the leather boots that lay there. If she waited any longer, she would run the risk of Tarah's parents arriving home before she had time to introduce herself. She gave her hair-covered toes one last wiggle of freedom before cramming them back into the confined space.

Without further hesitation, she exited the vehicle and began making her way across the grass. Fresh shivers of excitement ran through her as she reached the front entrance of the house, and she rubbed her hands together in anticipation.

Just as she reached up to knock, the door swung open in front of her, and Tarah stared out. Bav shot her hand to her neck as if startled, her fingers latching onto the talisman that dangled there. She took a step forward and reached out with her free hand.

Tarah's eyebrows rose. As she glanced at Bav's outstretched hand, a look of irritation spread across her face. "We don't want any." The girl stepped backward and slid her hand further up the door frame to swing it shut.

Bav lifted her bound foot into the opening to stop it from closing all the way. "Tarah, is it?" She peeked around the edge of the crack, searching Tarah's eyes. "I think you do."

The girl's grip loosened slightly on the door, "Do what?"

"Want it, of course."

Bav released her opal talisman as the girl opened the door back up the rest of the way. A look of confusion had settled onto her face, and Bav let out a low giggle, as if the girl was being ridiculous. She hoped the young woman's greedy nature would help to excuse the lack of explanation until the magic kicked in.

"What is it that you want to give me?"

"A prize, silly girl. Do you want it? I can only give it to you if you let me in, dear. Otherwise you forfeit and I look for someone else."

"I'm not sure letting you in is a good..." The spark in Tarah's eyes dimmed as she spoke, making it clear that the opal talisman was affecting her.

Bav interrupted, "That's a real pity. You have worked so hard, and I am quite sure that you deserve it. I mean, I would much prefer to give it to you than someone else."

"Of course, I want it." Tarah's smile returned, and she took a step back, ushering Bav to follow. Once inside, Bav swung the door closed behind her and thrust her arm out to the girl, this time grabbing Tarah's hand firmly, and she began shaking it vigorously as she spoke. "It's so great to meet you face-to-face." The skin on her palm tingled as the magic of the rune burned into the girl's flesh.

Tarah pulled her hand back with a sudden jerking motion, but Bav had anticipated the reaction and held fast. Her eyes grew wide as Bav's met them. They were no longer clouded over by the confusion spell, but that didn't matter anymore. It was too late to stop it.

Tarah opened her mouth wide, but before she could scream, Bav pulled her closer, whispering in her ear. "Don't bother, dear. The magic is already running through your veins." With her final word, she dropped the girl's hand and stepped away from her, clearing her throat as she moved.

"Magic? I don't believe in fairy tales, you weirdo. Get out of my house before I call the cops."

Bav smirked and look down at the girl's clenched fist. "Don't you want to see your prize first?"

"What kind of weird joke is this?"

"Look at your palm."

Bav watched as Tarah opened her hand and turned it over. Her brow tightened as she peered at the strange blue rune that covered her palm. She tried to rub the design away with her other hand, and Bav giggled.

"It won't wipe off, dear. It's your lesson. Your penance, you might say, and it can only be removed by your actions."

Tarah bolted from the room and around the corner, and the sound of running water hit Bav's ears. She slowly followed the noise to find Tarah scrubbing at her flesh with some sort of rough silver material that was near the sink. The action was quickly turning her skin a deep red.

"Now stop that before you hurt yourself."

Tarah looked up, and disbelief washed over her face. "Why are you still here? No, wait...stay, my parents will be here soon, and they will have you shipped straight off to an asylum!"

"Now, now, I doubt that, dear. They won't know I am here, and you aren't going to want me to go away when the transformation begins..."

Bav noted the girl's ashen complexion. Her top layers of skin were drying out, and flaky patches were growing even more apparent as the seconds passed.

"Transformation?" Tarah began to scratch at one of the patches unconsciously. "What are you yammering about?"

Bav pointed toward her. "Just have a look for yourself. Don't you see it starting already?"

Tarah's itching slowed, and her fingers twitched as she lifted them from her arm, revealing a shiny new layer of taut blue skin that had been uncovered in the spot where her nails had scratched the old layers off. A strangled gasp escaped her lips, and she backed up against the wall, holding the arm with the irregular blue splotches of skin out in front of her.

"In theory, the changes can be rather uncomfortable, and I wouldn't want you getting hurt."

"What have you done to me?"

"Now, don't blame me. You brought this on yourself. I merely did what you asked, and I believe I gave you just what you deserved. There's no turning back now. You're going to be the monster you behave like."

Bav glanced out the window. The natural light had all but vanished from the sky. "We should go to a more private location." Bav reached for her hand. "Let me help you to your room before your parents get home."

A tear slid down Tarah's cheek as Bav lightly clasped her fingers in her hand. "There is no use for that. It won't change anything."

Tarah moved ahead wordlessly to her room, closing her door behind them, and Bav wondered at her acceptance of the situation. She had been expecting more of a fight.

Tarah had sunk into a sitting position on the edge of her bed. She stared down at the rune on her palm. "Stop sulking, dear. You have a chance to learn a lesson here. You should be happy."

Tarah didn't look up. "I feel itchy everywhere." Bav could see fresh tears welling in her eyes. Pieces of dead skin were now falling off on their own, and they soon littered the surface of the bedspread.

Her throat suddenly felt tight, and she looked away from Tarah, examining the interior of the room. It offered her no comfort from her sudden guilt.

Her eyes passed over the door they had entered through and across the plain white walls that held no decorations. A second door hung open, and through it Bav could see that Tarah's powder room was kept the same way. These rooms had no character, no personality to speak of. "I have an idea. Why don't you go into your powder room over there and get cleaned up a bit?"

Tarah stood and moved toward the open door as if on autopilot. She looked up into Bav's eyes just before she silently swung the door closed.

With Tarah out of her sight, Bav released a sigh of relief. She needed a moment to compose herself.

She had been waiting to do this for so long. She needed to pull herself together. There was no place for pity. A faucet let out a screech from behind the closed door, and the sound of running water followed.

When Tarah reemerged, she had on crème-colored loose-fitting pants and a top of sorts; Bav assumed it was sleeping attire. Over it she wore a fluffy white robe. The ties hung free at her sides. Her red hair spilled around her shoulders, and Bav stared in awe at her creation. "That didn't work out how I expected, did it?"

"What do you mean?"

"You are a lovely creature."

"I am a monster, just like you said." Tarah moved the side of her robe and lifted the bottom of her shirt a few inches against her ribs to reveal a newly emerging limb. The small arm and hand that protruded below her ribcage seemed to be getting larger by the second. "There's one on each side." Tarah choked out the words.

"I could think of many uses a nonmagical would have for a few extra arms." Bav crinkled her nose. "To each their own. It's probably for the best that you feel that way anyhow."

Tarah's eyes were still locked on the growing nub as she spoke. "What did I do to deserve this!"

She knew that the girl didn't expect an answer.

Tarah looked up, locking her eyes onto Bav's, and opened her mouth to say something else, but before she could utter a sound, Bav beat her to it. "Now, don't make excuses. I told you that won't help. Come sit down and relax. Your transformation is almost complete. It's what I have dreamed of for so long."

"You said in theory, before and now...am I some kind of experiment? Your guinea pig?"

"No." Bav shook her head violently at the accusation. "I want you to learn, and learn you will." She patted the place on the bed next to her, and Tarah reluctantly lowered herself to sit beside her.

"You thought stories of magic came purely from human imagination, did you? That is not the case." Bav cocked her head to the side. She couldn't believe Tarah was still sulking.

Tarah stared down at her feet, and Bav snapped her fingers to get her attention before continuing. "I'm sure that somewhere down the line, humans continued to tell of magic after the realms sprouted. The stories morphed and changed but never disappeared entirely. As much as the goddesses would have wanted them to."

Tarah shook her head and turned her face toward the wall.

"There is much about this world that you don't know. The magical races have been hidden from humans for hundreds and hundreds of years."

Tarah's eyes remained trained on the wall as she folded her arms over her chest. "Do you really expect me to believe anything you say?"

"It really doesn't matter what you believe or don't. I'm still going to tell you."

Tarah sighed and turned her face back to Bav as she continued.

"The arcane, the jinn, humans, we all used to live together here, locked in a never-ending battle for dominance between the magical races. It was a hard life for some. She looked up into Tarah's eyes. "I never really fit in with my kind, even when I was a little girl."

"Instead of hunting jinn, as I was supposed to, when I was a youth I had been drawn to the humans. When Sophia created the veil to separate the realms and stop the magical species from interacting with each other and her human creations, my fun, my purpose, was brought to an end."

"If that is at all true, then how are you here now?"

She shrugged back at Tarah, although the question caused her to pause and think. She hadn't bothered to worry about the how or the why at the time. "I saw a strange shimmering mist in front of me and simply walked through. I didn't much care about the reasons. I left the settlements and cities in my realm behind long ago. Imagine my delight at finding myself back with the humans, where I belong."

Tarah buried her face in her pillow to stifle a scream of frustration, and again Bav pitied the teen. She wondered if she had fully considered the consequences of introducing magic back into a place that hadn't seen a speck of it for hundreds of years.

Bav furrowed her brow as her thoughts returned to the first pupil she had tried to acquire after she arrived in the human realm. There had been something...

A loud knock at the door caused them both to leap up from the bed. Bav grabbed at her talisman, softly whispering to it as Tarah tied the sash of her robe tightly around her waist and tiptoed toward the door, opening it only a crack.

A shrill voice reached Bav's ears, causing her to wince.

"Tarah, there is a mess."

"A mess?" She spoke in a low voice, barely audible to Bav's ears.

"Don't you play dumb with me. You know that this house needs to be kept clean and in order! I will not tolerate imperfection."

"I am sorry, I'm just...not well."

"Come out here and apologize properly!"

"I'm probably contagious. I wouldn't want to subject you to my germs."

"Open that door up this instant."

Bav watched in silence as Tarah removed her hand from the knob, allowing the door to swing open. The woman on the other side gaped at the sight of Tarah as she backed away and into the wall. "What are you trying to do to me? Just you wait until your father gets home." The woman spun around, hurrying away, and Bav scratched at her chin, bewildered at what had just played out.

"Take it back, Bav. Please, you don't know what they will do."

"I cannot."

She turned back to face Bav, closing the door silently as she moved.

"Then use your magic to hide me like you did for yourself."

"There are safeguards in the spell I used to transform you. It would stop you from hiding."

Tarah's eyes grew wide. "You said you didn't want me hurt!"

"If you could use magic to hide, it would ruin the lesson."

Tarah crossed her arms over her chest and turned to stare out her window.

"Now, don't you think you're being a little dramatic?"

Tarah turned her face back to Bav, and the look in her eyes caused goosebumps to rise on her arms.

"You need to get me out of here. Now."

Bav was dumbstruck, but she reached for Tarah's hand.

The house was still as they made their way to the entrance and opened the door to the outside.

Tarah's mother and a tall, lanky man were on the edge of the lawn, talking in hushed tones. The man, Tarah's father she assumed, turned visibly paler and grimaced.

Tarah's grip tightened on Bav's hand as the pair turned their faces to look at them. Tarah's mother pointed at the doorway where they stood and raised her voice. "See for yourself."

"I am not blind." The man gulped. "They will be here any minute."

Bav pulled at Tarah's hand, but she seemed frozen, like a fawn caught in a sudden bright light. She wrinkled her nose and reached for her talisman, just as a plain white van sped past and then reversed to stop next to Tarah's parents. Two men jumped from the vehicle. Before Bav could form a coherent thought, they rushed toward her pupil.

A sudden loud crack of lightning filled the bright sky above them as one of the men latched his arm around Tarah's waist and tried to pull her away. Bav felt her fingers slipping out of her hand and then lurched backward as she lost her grasp.

Unseen, Bav followed behind the pair toward the open van door. Tarah clawed and kicked at the hulking men in desperation. As Bav neared the struggling trio, another lightning bolt exploded above them.

The air felt heavy, and Bav's skin prickled as the world in front of her began to seem out of focus. It was as if a haze had suddenly descended in front of her.

She heard Tarah scream and gasp. She could feel her hands grabbing at her, then being pulled away once again, but something else had caught her attention.

Bav didn't dare look away from the spectacle. Her heart pounded in her chest as she whispered, "I'm not ready to go." She reached up to clutch her talisman, but she felt only bare skin at her neckline, skin that was rapidly becoming wrinkled and dry.

The world in front of her wavered as a long green tentacle reached forward out of the foggy haze. Some creature was coming through the veil, just as she had.

A second tentacle slipped through, stretching out in her direction. Bav summoned up every ounce of energy she had and tore her eyes from the monster, spinning around on her heels. But her aged muscles didn't cooperate the way she expected them to.

Just as the sound of the van doors slamming shut hit her ears, she felt the slimy creature's appendages brush across her flesh.

A sick slurping sound filled her ears, as if the thing was tasting her.

She could feel the creature's suction cups pressing into her skin. In her aged state, she had no way to fight back. Bav bellowed toward the van as a muscular tentacle secured itself around her waist, "This isn't how it was supposed to go."

Bav craned her neck. She would have lost her invisibility when she lost her talisman, but the men from the van had been too preoccupied with the struggling Tarah to have noticed her appear out of thin air, and the parents where nowhere to be seen.

She clenched her jaw. She had no doubt that they had taken their leave before the men even reached their daughter.

Bav hoped the girl could manage without her. She had no idea when or how she would get back to the human realm. She wasn't even sure where she was going, because nothing like the tentacled creature that was dragging her body through the veil lived in the arcane realm.

III

Day 32,854

Amma Part One ~ The Escape

Amma wasn't supposed to be here.

She had run so far and so fast that she barely registered where she had ended up at the moment she emerged from the shelter of the trees. She stopped moving as bright light surrounded her and her feet sank into hot, dry sand. Her left hand felt weighed down, and she realized she was still gripping the rock. She loosened her fingers until it fell from her hand and rolled forward, collecting sand on the sticky parts of its surface as it moved.

At first, all she could hear was the echoes of her own heart as it thundered while she gasped for breath, sucking in hot air. It still felt as if her body was propelling forward, even though she had quit running.

She held her shaking hands in front of her and stared at them, unbelieving, as she collapsed to her knees in the gritty sand with her head bent down and her eyes closed tight.

When her heart rate slowed, the slapping of the waves became predominant. The wind made a steady swooshing noise in her ears. It reminded her of the sound that emanated from the one precious conch they had within the village when you blew into it.

Her voice was as unsteady as her hands as she whispered, "I'm not supposed to be here."

She clutched her shaking palms together on her lap and raised her chin. Her eyes darted around, and a new kind of panic began to settle in under her skin.

There were reasons why her village was tucked away deep in the center of the island, hidden from the sea that surrounded them. Reasons why they never ventured to the shore or rarely even left the perimeter of their dreary territory.

They were hiding from whatever lived beneath the waves.

Monsters.

Amma hadn't meant to end up here, but now that she had, there would be no simple way to turn back.

They had a route they were supposed to follow, just in case the creatures ever wandered onto the shore, precautions to keep them away from the villagers and intricate paths to follow that were said to throw them off the scent of humans.

And they must have worked, for no one had encountered one of the creatures in ages, that she knew of. Certainly not before she, or her mother for that matter, had been born. In fact, it had been so long that some of the people from the village had started to doubt they existed at all.

Amma knew better. There was a logical basis for the rules. Things had happened in the past. It was why her mother had instilled a fear of water in her since birth. The same fear that had been etched deep into her own mother's subconscious by the words of her grandmother.

It was why her grandmother's parents had worked so hard to make leaving the village almost unnecessary and the reason none of the children born there had ever been taught to swim.

Her great-grandparents and the other survivors of the fall had replanted fruit trees and various types of edible roots in the center of where their town now stood, constructing hovels of stone, mud, and plants in an orderly fashion around the field of sustenance.

Although fresh water in the form of rainfall was collected on roofs and catchments to be stored for later use, they had also dug into the only freshwater river on the island, expanding it to encircle the perimeter, creating a protective boarder of sorts. It was not only a source of drinkable water but also a reminder not to stray.

They constructed one small wooden bridge at the very point where the original river had once ended.

Amma often stood still on that bridge, listening to the stream gurgling and sloshing below as the rushing water met the slower-flowing shallow edges of the hand-dug banks. Leaving the village for anything other than the pursuit of fresh meat was a forbidden act. This rule, they were taught, was vital for their continued survival.

Even in her present state of shock, she smiled at the thought of fresh meat. Such a luxury was rare. The only animals that roamed the interior of the island were poisonous lizards, bats, and the occasional curious bird.

The acres that surrounded them beyond the fresh water were cluttered with cedar and palm trees. The moss that grew in their shade imparted an itchy and painful rash. Anywhere the light managed to peek through the canopy and reach the ground would be covered with snaking vines and fronds that would curl around your ankles if you stood stock-still for too long.

Amma breathed in deeply. As she exhaled, bitterness filled her mouth. The air tasted different here.

The island had always seemed large to her, but until now she had nothing to compare it with. Here at the edge of the great sea, it seemed a speck in comparison to the cerulean blue water that surrounded it.

The pink sand burned at the soles of her bare feet, and she took several steps closer to the shoreline until her toes landed on the darker damp area at the sea's edge. As her feet sank into the thick mud, it reminded her of the mixture they used to rebuild their hovels when they started to wear down.

Her stomach growled, and she licked at her dry lips, unsure whether it was caused by hunger or fear. She turned in a slow circle, not knowing what she was looking for.

She wasn't sure what the monsters looked like; no one alive was. They were always deemed indescribable horrors.

When her eyes made it back to the gentle waves, she let out a haggard breath and then scolded herself again.

"You are not supposed to be here."

Amma found it difficult to tear her eyes from the sight for a second time. She was enthralled by the rhythm of the lapping waves and the glimmer of the sun beating down on the endless sea that spread out in front of her. Biding her time, she drank in the foreign world.

Since they weren't permitted to romp around the island freely, she had never seen it before; it just wasn't allowed. But she had run so fast and so far, forgetting everything she had been taught, and now that she was here, she couldn't just turn and run back to that place.

Even if she wasn't punished for what she had done, if she simply headed back from her roost here on the shore, whatever was out there hidden below the surface could follow.

Amma lurched forward, dipping a finger into the edge of a wave as it rolled close to her, and then raised it to her mouth. She licked at it, and her face contorted in disgust. This water tasted funny, like the air that swirled around her, hot, heavy, and salty. Different.

Something coarse and wet brushed against her foot, and she let out a shriek as she stumbled backward, landing hard on the hot sand.

She caught a brief glimpse of the animal before her teeth knocked together and her eyes squeezed shut from the impact.

The creature's hard exoskeleton was a dull orange, like the bitter, round fruits she sometimes added to the skewer when cashew apples and bananas were scarcer.

Could this small thing be the monster that had driven her grandparents into hiding?

When she pushed her eyelids open, the animal was staring back at her, point-blank, with its beady, red-tinged eyes.

Amma heaved backward in the sand, thinking it was perhaps sizing her up. The animal's antenna twitched as it peered at her, raising its pair of claws in her direction.

She knew better than to judge the animal by its small size alone. On the island, danger came in all shapes.

The animal lifted one claw higher and seemed to be aiming at her face as it moved sideways toward her on ten jointed legs. It appeared ready to attack.

Amma reached behind herself, blindly searching for a weapon, much as she had the night before, but when her hand bumped into the rock, she pulled it back in horror.

The crustacean let out a low hissing and scuttled backward until a wave washed over it and dragged it back out into the sea.

Something in her reaction must have scared the animal, Amma thought as she swallowed hard. Her lips felt dry, her throat scratchy. She brushed her hair back from her face as she shifted into a sitting position and pulled her knees up to her chest.

She deserved this torment of not knowing.

Fresh tears prickled at the corners of her eyes as her thoughts returned to the rock.

Last night's attack had not been the first she had endured, but it was the most brutal. She knew that this was in part because she had fought back with everything she had. When that didn't work, she wiggled and clawed at the ground until her hand had landed on the rock.

The rest was a blur in her mind. She knew that she had brought it down on his head more than once before pushing her attacker off and staggering forward. She didn't remember looking down to check his condition. All she could think to do was run, and she had fled, out of fear that he would get up and attack again.

The rock had saved her and allowed her to escape, but escape to what?

She stood back up but was unsure which way to go. To her left, sand continued to blanket the island's edge, and to the right the shoreline of the beach transformed into a rock-covered canvas. She spun to the left, choosing the path with the fewest obstacles, and teetered as she took the next step forward.

There had been a flash of brown and white in her peripheral vision as a large sea bird swooped down and tried to lift something up from the water's surface. The wild frenzy of flapping wings drew her attention skyward and back above the vast ocean.

Amma didn't shriek in terror at the unfamiliar sight this time. But the wings flapping in a violent manic way caused her to gasp and step back again.

She had seen birds on occasion. Curious, they would fly and land near the village, but they had been much smaller, much more colorful creatures, often with feathers of bright orange, red, and green. Colors the inhabitants of the island only wished they could replicate.

Her heart, like the bird's powerful wings, rapped in her chest. Whatever it had lunged for, the bird had failed to retrieve, and she couldn't help but wonder if this could be the creature that had taken so many of the originals' lives after the fall.

The sea bird swooped forward then down, diving toward the water once again. Amma raised a hand to her throat, startled by the quickness of its movements. As she did so, she felt the top of her dress flop open a few inches farther down from the neckline than was normal.

A frown came to her lips. In last night's attack, she had lost one of the precious buttons used to hold her dress closed.

She didn't dare to take her eyes off the bird as the thought registered. She lowered her hand back to her side just as she saw the bird rise again from the ocean. The long, slender creature in its beak was not dangling limply but flailing and fighting hard to be released.

The bird's prey was ropelike, only its head had a flatter appearance. Its scales shimmered in the rays of light as it twisted and flung itself back and forth, trying to escape. Its long, cylindrical body was covered in rings of stripes, both yellow and blue.

By its shear length, it was a wonder that it couldn't free itself. The captive seemed to be at least twice as long as the carrion bird that held it in its beak.

The bird continued to hold strong as it maneuvered its prisoner toward the rocky side of the shore before beginning its descent. It didn't release the creature until it gave up and stopped fighting. As the bird raised its beak in her direction, she saw the hook-shaped end of its mouth that had impaled the animal. The bird paid her little mind as it began pecking at its kill.

The sea bird wasn't after her either.

Amma looked away in disgust.

Noticing for the first time that the moon had disappeared from its place next to the ever-present sun, she bent down, recalling what she had written yesterday in the ash of her cooled fire pit: 32851.

She wrote 32852 in the sand at her feet. It was a new day, after all.

It had once been a custom shared between everyone to measure the passing time this way. But at one point, the rest of the village had stopped. That was thousands of days ago.

It was hard to believe that so much time had passed by since her mother died. Only she continued to count. She would trace the numbers in places where they would be quick to disappear, keeping the permanent tally in a secret location within her own mind.

The others had called it a useless tradition. A remnant of a world none of them had ever known firsthand, a world where the sun and the moon played out a systematic dance within a twenty-four-hour period.

Amma didn't like the idea of it, the sun disappearing at night. It was the only story of the old world that made her glad to be here.

She wiped the back of her hand against her tear-streaked cheeks. So much had changed since her mother died. They had feared her, at least to a point, due to the things she knew, even though she wouldn't utter them out loud to a soul, beyond her daughter.

She had been too hurt by the past.

Amma stood upright and kicked at the numbers, making them disappear before changing direction. She would move along the right side of the island. She would take the more perilous route.

As she moved forward, she tried to focus on the rocks in her path, but her mind kept wandering back to the memories of her mother.

She would tell her stories of places and creatures beyond her imagination. Often the tales would come out of her mouth unprovoked as they stared into the dancing flames of the fire just outside their hut.

Amma would be sitting curled up in her lap while her mother combed her fingers through her hair. She would stiffen each time her mother would pause the movement of her hand, knowing she was about to be embraced too tightly, then her mother would begin whispering in her ear.

Each time she would start by saying, "Don't repeat what I say, but don't forget either. They don't deserve to know. The lot of them."

She knew her mother wasn't trying to be cruel when she tugged at her locks, rather trying to reinforce her words.

The psychological exercise had worked better than she had hoped. Even now, when the villagers tried to ask her about the world away from here, Amma would freeze, remembering only how her mother had taught her not to say a thing.

Amma knew it was part of the reason they treated her so poorly. They thought that she was withholding information to spite them. The truth was, it had been drilled into her head for so long that when she tried to recall the stories out loud, she only managed to stutter unintelligibly.

Amma paused. In front of her, the rocks began to jut up at odd angles, and as the open water hit them in waves, it sprayed out around them, making them slippery in appearance.

She turned to move inland, where the thick slabs of rock still lay flatter against the shore, but as she did, a warning caw filled her ears.

Her mouth gaped open at the sight. She had been so deep in thought that she hadn't noticed the nests of sticks and seaweed that speckled the landscape beside her. Amma could see that the cluster of sea birds was not identical. It appeared as if multiple species had banded together in unity to roost safely amongst these rocks.

The roost closest to her held a large brown-and-white bird, similar to the one she had seen earlier scavenging for food. Now, as she looked at it, the bird spread its wings and puffed out its chest, cautioning her not to approach. In seconds, the birds within the nests beyond that began imitating its response, and her ears filled with their piercing warning cries.

Amma turned back to the jutting rocks, knowing the birds would be impassible. As she moved forward, she was careful to watch where her feet fell. Slimy green moss flourished amid the stones, and she tried to avoid contact with their surfaces in particular. Before long, the spray of the waves soaked her clothing, causing it to cling to her skin and making it difficult to maneuver her legs. By the time she heaved herself over the last jutting rock and onto a pebbled shore below, she was exhausted.

She sprawled out on the ground and stared up into the sky. The moon had reappeared beside the sun. Her skin prickled. She had been moving all day, but toward what? Lacking the shade of the trees and thick foliage of their village, the heat of the rays felt different here, harsher. Although her clothing dried fast under the duel lights, her exposed skin grew hot in a very uncomfortable way.

She sat up. She couldn't stay here in the open. Her heart ached at the thought of leaving the shore, but she pushed herself back up onto her feet. The ocean was a seductress, and it had successfully seduced her.

It seemed odd now that she hadn't ever stood here before. Even though she had never known a different life, it felt wrong the way they lived. The village was a prison, and this felt like freedom. The first she had ever known.

She made her way to the tree line, but just close enough that the shadows of the branches blocked most of the rays from the sun and moon.

Amma continued to move along the edge of the island until the pebbles again gave way to softer sand. At that point, her legs became shaky from the lack of rest, and she had no choice but to lower herself to the ground.

When she woke, the air felt hot and dry as the warm breeze blew over her sand-encrusted skin. She had fallen asleep sitting against a tree's thick trunk. Her muscles cried out as she pushed herself forward, crawling on her hands and knees to the waterline. Without much thought, she bent over and brought her face in close. She barely recognized the blistered features that reflected back at her as she moved to douse her face with the water. A stinging sensation engulfed her cheeks and nose. She pulled back, crying in shock at her skin's reaction. She covered her face with her hands, but the pressure only made the pain worse.

She hung her head, allowing her hair to fan out around her face, and took in a deep breath, waiting for the pain to subside.

When she looked up again, a tear-shaped creature was emerging from the water.

Its carapace was covered by skin and oily flesh that went from dark gray to black and had a scattering of white blotches. Seven ridges ran the length of the animal's back.

Its head, although bigger than her own, appeared to be too small for its large body as it stretched its neck in her direction and stared at her with green-rimmed eyes.

Amma stiffened and stared back, trying to determine if she saw bloodlust in its gaze and wondering what the animal was capable of.

The creature didn't appear to have teeth, but the points on the upper lip of its beaked mouth were serrated. Amma knew it could easily tear through her flesh.

Its long, narrow front flippers seemed almost wing like to Amma, and when they began to move again, she covered her eyes in fright, thinking the thing was going to fly at her. When the seconds ticked by and she didn't feel the wind rush past her or the weight of the animal bearing down on her, she peeked between her fingers.

The creature had lost interest in her and was using its flippers to push the dirt away from beneath it. Amma lowered her arms back down into her lap and watched the immense animal work.

As it dug deeper, the animal began to make its way into the hole, and she could see that it had shorter hind flippers and a small pointed tail at its rear.

Still afraid to make any sudden movements and startle the animal, she pulled her knees up to her chest and wrapped her arms around them.

She watched in fascination as the reptile proceeded to lay eggs and then cover them over. It didn't seem to pay her any further mind throughout the process, as if it had forgotten she was there at all. When it finished smoothing the sand over its newly lain eggs, it turned and headed back into the sea, quickly disappearing beneath the water.

Amma shook her head and released a cautious giggle. The animal had come to shore only to construct a place to lay eggs. Her belly rumbled as she thought of the bird eggs she had eaten once, then her mind wandered to her mother. The animal that laid them was not a bird. If anything, Amma thought it was more closely related to the lizards they hunted for meat on the inland.

The pain from the poison of the lizards was very real. She had watched her mother suffer through it before her death. It was a horrible way to die. Her features had become gaunt and her eyes hollow as the poison made its way through her system.

The lizards rarely attacked unless provoked. Eggs had been what she was after when it happened.

As Amma had grown and her mother witnessed the steady decline in the villagers, she had relented and tried to help them. She knew that if things went on the way they were, Amma would have no future.

She had found notes stuffed in the seam of the old suitcase that lay useless on their hovel's floor. Thoughts jotted down by her great-grandparents before they died.

In the old world, they had been people of science. It was why their knowledge had been so useful to the other survivors.

Their hypothesis was that if they collected the eggs from one of the lizards, they could raise their own within the village and reduce the risk associated with hunting outside the barrier. They even had a rough idea of how the venom sacks could easily and safely be removed while the lizards were still young.

Amma had begged her not to go. She tried to remind her of the torment the villagers had put her through when her own mother had died. How they had stolen into her home and taken the books left by her grandparents in order to destroy them.

How they had wanted to rid themselves of the past once and for all.

"They have learned better now; I see the desperation in their eyes. I have to forgive, for your sake."

She explained further. "Once the village was built and my grandparents had done all they thought they could do, life settled into a routine here. The hope of rescue diminished by the day, and most of the original survivors died off by the time my mother made it to your age. A decree was made no longer to speak of the past.

"Their thought was that the youth couldn't miss or long for things that they never knew existed. They needed to adapt to survive in this harsh environment, and the memories and thoughts of rescue were holding them back.

"Your great-grandparents didn't agree with the decision, but they had to protect their daughter. By the time your grandmother had me, her parents had grown wrinkled with age."

"Wrinkled?" Amma had crinkled her nose at her words; she couldn't picture it.

"They were probably the first and last to die on the island from old age. You know it was uninhabited by humans when they arrived."

Amma crawled forward to the spot where the animal had just been. She glanced out at the water, wondering if the animal would return to protect its young. When she was sure the creature was no longer anywhere near, she proceeded. She would only take enough to sustain her for the day.

When she uncovered the eggs, she found there had to be at least a hundred of the things. They looked nothing like the bird eggs she had eaten. The shells were not hard ovals, but soft-looking and rather rounded. They were surrounded by a thick, clear mucus.

She reached into the cavity and grabbed for one. It covered about half of her palm, and its shell felt leathery in texture.

She tore it open and lifted it over her face to let the contents drip into her mouth. She closed her eyes as she swallowed. She had eaten worse-looking things.

Amma covered the eggs back over the way the animal had before she rose to her feet to continue her wandering trek. As her feet left a trail of impressions in the gritty sand behind her, she wondered how long it would be before she would have made a circle around the island.

The hair on the back of her neck bristled with the ludicrous thought, and she wrapped her arms over her stomach as she continued forward.

Like Amma, her mother was born here, but her grandmother had come here at a young age, little more than an infant. It had been a miracle she had survived the fall and the exploration as she had. Luckier still, both her parents had survived as well. Many other children older than her had not fared so well.

Amma wished she had known her great-grandparents. She couldn't even imagine what it would have been like to hear the tales of the outside world and the arrival here, as her grandmother had learned them, straight from those who experienced it.

She also would have liked to be able to learn to read from the collection of books her great-grandparents had brought with them to the island, as her own mother had, but by the time she was born they had already been destroyed.

Being their only written sources of information about where they had come from, her grandparents had fought to keep the books from harm, sometimes even sacrificing the safety of others to protect them from destruction. This earned them respect from some but jealousy and hatred among others.

And fear, of course, Amma thought.

That fear had kept the villagers at a distance, for a time.

Her mother had never divulged to Amma how it happened. But the aftermath of her grandmother's death was a subject she brought up again and again.

It was at that period, between her grandmother's death and her own birth, that the discussions of the old world had been forbidden.

What fear the others had held dwindled after her grandmother's passing, and they had taken the books, burning them.

By the time they saw error in their actions and repented, she refused to share the knowledge that had been passed down to her.

It was the very reason Amma's mother had whispered the warnings into her ear, insisting that they didn't deserve the knowledge anyway.

Devastated, it had taken almost her entire lifetime to get over the intrusion, the destruction.

Then, later, before she was driven delirious from the pain and fever of the lizard's venom, Amma's mother had revealed another fear etched into her by her grandmother.

It seemed she had held the belief that if all was forgotten about the civilization they came from, it was inevitable that they would regress, and lawlessness would prevail.

After revealing this, her mother had insisted that she could see it happening, day by day, and had for a while.

Amma hadn't realized it until now, but her mother had been right, and so had her grandmother. Things had turned out as they feared.

Amma dropped her arms to her sides and stood still. If she made the trek around the island and survived, she could offer them the knowledge that she learned along the way. Perhaps, she thought, she would find her voice when she wasn't repeating her mother, but rather reciting her own tale of exploration.

And maybe, she hoped, there was a chance they wouldn't treat her the way they did, and she could draw up the courage to explain what her mother had been trying to accomplish when she was bitten. If she could pull it off, she could earn their respect.

For a moment, an electric excitement flashed through her, making her arms and legs tingle with the thought, but as she felt a wild grin spread over her face, the image of the man she had fled from crept to the surface of her memory.

His grotesque features. Dry and cracked lips coming toward her as he tried to keep her pinned to the ground. The uncaring look in his eyes as she struggled. The way he seemed to squeal with delight each time her arm managed to slip loose, because he knew she was stuck, weighed down by the sheer force of his body on her small frame.

Amma looked down at her feet and took a deep breath, no longer sure that she desired their respect. She wasn't even sure if she wanted to return at all. Surely a life by the sea offered her more of an opportunity to live, even if she risked everything by remaining here.

She took another step forward and then another, continuing her journey. There was nothing else she could do.

When the giant metal body came into view, Amma stopped and stared at it. It was a thing of myth from her mother's stories, and yet it stretched before her from the shore to the edge of the tree line. An almost forgotten legend.

How many more generations before it was completely wiped from the other villagers' minds?

As Amma again began to move closer, she could see that the 747 wasn't the only man-made thing here. The land surrounding the flying machine was littered with a blanket of debris. Each of the unnatural items seemed to be covered in a different amount of sand, rust, and seaweed, as if someone had dumped human waste in this spot over and over again for an eternity.

Some of the items were so shiny that as the sun reflected off them, they shone back with an intensity that made her eyes water.

Amma kicked at one rectangular contraption with her foot, toppling it onto its side. Beneath it she uncovered a curious wristband with a circle at its center. Within the circle, numbers rimmed its cracked face in sequential order from one to twelve. Two arrows, one small and one larger, both rested pointing up at the twelve. A trinket from a world unknown to her. Amma tossed the relic back down and raised her eyes to the tree line before making her way toward it.

Two deep trenches marred the ground near the outer trees. Amma couldn't tell if the crevasses were natural or hand-dug, but a flat wooden board had been shoved into the ground between them. The numbers 05, 12, and 45 were carved into it, one below the other. She searched her memory, but in that order the numbers meant nothing to her.

Amma peered down into the holes. What looked like pieces of torn cloth were all that was visible at the bottoms. The material was a faded green and looked considerably thicker than the cloth of her dress. Perhaps, Amma thought, something once buried had been dug back up. Or maybe it had never gotten the chance to be buried.

A shiver ran through her as she looked back up and directed her eyes into the trees. Beyond the forest's edge, a wing of another type of flying machine protruded from the ground.

She stepped gingerly by one of the empty holes and peeked in under the canopy. This machine was much smaller than the 747. It had a propeller in the front that reminded her somewhat of the design for the pinwheel plaything her mother had made for her from parts of the thorny weeds that grew in the shaded areas by the rivers bank.

Each wing that stretched out from its sides held the image of a star within a circle. The design of this plane looked much simpler to Amma, as if it had come from an earlier time, and yet at first glance, it appeared to be in relatively better condition than the larger aircraft.

Amma wasn't surprised by the sight of the machine. She knew others had come after the original fall.

She had even once heard what her mother had said was the roar of an engine in the dead of the night. Curious, she had run for the door of the hut.

Amma breathed in deeply and sighed as she closed her eyes, listening to the rhythmic lapping of the waves and her thoughts plummet into the past.

As she replayed the memory, the hair at the nap of her neck prickled. The air that moved across her exposed skin felt lighter, as if the world around her was changing with her thoughts. She could still hear the waves on the shore, but she also swore she could smell a hint of the smoke from the firepit that smoldered outside the door to the hovel that she shared with her mom.

It felt as if she were in both places at once.

Part of the sky above the trees was visible, and Amma could see the red and orange glow of fire within it. Her mom grabbed at her, tugging her arm, trying to get her back inside.

She heard the loud noise of crashing trees as the plane plummeted to the ground in the distance.

"I want to go see; I want to help."

She had still been young and had not yet seen the villagers' cruelty firsthand. She was innocent then. Amma wondered where the other villagers were, and her eyes went wide. Surely, they had heard the commotion.

"Going there will make it worse," her mother whispered as she knelt beside her, still gripping her arm.

Amma looked up into her eyes. "They might be able to take us away from here."

"No Amma." She shook her head. "They won't."

"Maybe we can help."

"There is nothing we can do, and you will put all of us, me included, in danger."

Amma's eyes were still fixed on her mother as she felt a tear roll down her cheek. She shivered at her mother's light touch as she brushed it away before speaking again.

"You must stand back and protect yourself when there's nothing you can do to help."

Disappointment had filled her at her mother's words, but Amma stopped fighting, and when her mother had finally managed to pull her inside, they huddled together in silence and listened to the eerie quiet of the island.

If the passengers of that craft had survived, they had never made it to the village, and Amma had never brought the incident up again.

Amma turned away from the wreckage; the other plane was what she was interested in. As she approached, the sound of the waves seemed to grow louder, and thoughts of the stories her mom once told her about the fall twisted in her head, pulling her toward the 747 with curiosity and rising terror.

The flying machine was a sight to behold. Even though she had been told the plane had held hundreds of passengers, she wasn't prepared to take in its enormous size. The aircraft, like the sound of the waves, seemed to grow the closer she got.

Unlike the smaller aircraft, corrosion had caused the body to be almost entirely covered in dull white and gray patches, except where cracks in the metal were visible. In those areas, even at a distance, Amma could see a brownish orange residue of some sort clinging to and radiating out from the fractures.

Amma tapped her finger thoughtfully against her chin and decided the exterior was in better shape than she would have expected after nine decades. After all, their hovels had to be replaced every thousand days or so.

Questions she had no way of getting the answers to flitted through her. She wondered how long the survivors had waited here after the storm brought the metal giant down. Had only days passed before they had realized no one would be coming to rescue them and that they would have to create a new life for themselves? How long before they had learned of the monsters and moved from here?

Wind and weather had piled sand up against its side, and Amma walked up the incline before reaching forward with one hand and placing it against the rough metal. She leaned in close, trying to peek through one of the windows, but the view inside was distorted by the grime.

She removed her hand and took several steps backward. The front of the plane, which faced the tree line, seemed intact, but unlike the smaller plane, there was no visible tail at the back of this one. She decided to make a wide circle around its body.

As Amma made her way around it, just a few feet from the water's edge, she was met by a large hole at the end of the structure. It appeared to her as if the tail of the aircraft had been ripped clean off.

The opening was higher up than Amma could reach, but a spiral-shaped staircase was propped against the gaping hole. She gripped the rail and made her way up to the place where the floor and the staircase touched.

She took a step onto the relic, and a shiver ran up her spine. White bones were broken and scattered on the deck floor among the rubbish.

From the shapes of them, they looked human. Amma rubbed the goosebumps on her arms and raised her eyes to the pairs of seats that lined the walls on each side. Most of them appeared to be empty.

The second chair on her right held a rectangular book, but the cover was not hard like the ones her mom had described. Amma picked it up and ran her fingers over the image on the front. The right side had been damaged by water, but on the left, a woman's face protruded from the cover, her delicate features became smudged halfway across the page. At the top the letters VOG were still legible, and directly below the letters was a symbol Amma didn't recognize. It reminded her of a small s, but two thin lines ran through the letter from top to bottom. It was positioned next to a large number one. Below that, "DEC" was printed. Amma attempted to flip the pages, but the mildewy residue caused them to stick together. She set it gently back down into the seat and moved forward between the rows until she reached the front row.

Ahead of her was what appeared to be a rectangular door, although she didn't see a handle to pull it open. Amma pressed her body against it and pushed as hard as she could, but it didn't budge. She backed up, staring hard at the door as she moved to lower herself down onto one of the cushioned seats in the first row. As her flesh met the fabric, something hard bit into her thigh, causing her to spring forward in shock. She stiffened and sucked in her breath as she whipped her body around to investigate her attacker.

As her eyes met the thing on the seat, she dropped her shoulders and released the air from her lungs. Amma bent down, picked up the small, arm-shaped object, and looked at it. It wasn't made of flesh and bone. It was smooth to the touch and only as long as her palm. At one end of the arm there was a rounded joint, and at the other it resembled a baby's hand with its tiny fingers curled into a fist.

Amma furrowed her brow, wondering if it was a piece of a child's plaything. She gripped the plastic arm tight in her fingers as fresh tears prickled the corners of her eyes.

Was she going to have a baby?

Her stomach knotted at the thought, and she wrapped her arms around it, still clinging to the lifelike fragment as the tears started to stream down her hot, raw cheeks.

Her throat constricted as bile rose from her stomach.

Amma turned away with a jerk and bolted toward the staircase. Instead of climbing down, she jumped off the edge and landed with a painful thud in the sand. She leaned forward as a gagging noise emitted from her mouth and the small amount of food she had eaten forced its way up and out.

Amma stood, wiping at her mouth with her free hand. Relieved to be out of the vessel, she assured herself that she wouldn't find answers there anyway; she didn't even know what most of the things on board were.

She opened her fist and looked at the toy again. What would be waiting for her if she returned to the village with nothing?

Death would be better.

As the thought registered, she dropped the plastic arm and turned toward the sea.

Amma's steps felt lighter when she began walking into the water. As the liquid moved over her feet, ankles, and then her hips, another memory of her mother emerged. She paused, allowing a wave to wash over her. She imagined her mother kneeling in front of her before placing a hand on her chest. "The ocean beats in a rhythm similar to this, but it has no heart."

Amma responded to the memory by pushing herself forward and whispering, "Then I will give it mine."

The water seemed to respond to her words by tugging at her, beckoning her forward, then just as swiftly a new wave appeared, bigger than the last, threatening to make her fall backward as it crashed into her. She clenched her toes and dug them into the sand. When the wave hit, she gritted her teeth and pushed herself into it as it tumbled toward her, splashing her face and spraying out over her head. The water felt impossibly cool on her skin as it trickled down.

She balled her fists at her sides and waited for the water to retreat, determined to allow it to pull her out into the deep. As it did, she propelled her body into it with all the energy she could muster.

The impact knocked the air from her lungs as the water turned her, tearing at her thin clothing. Amma felt an urge run through her to move her arms and legs, but she forced them to remain limp as she was moved away from the shore.

As the intensity of the waters pull lessened, Amma felt herself lifting back toward the surface, instead of sinking in deeper as she had intended, and she wondered if the ocean was rejecting her. Her chest burned with a desire to breathe, and she sucked in to allow the liquid to fill her greedy lungs, just as her head popped back above the water. The mixture of liquid and air that entered her gaping mouth caused her chest to clench painfully, and she began to cough in uncontrollable bursts as her head bobbed up in down in the now-still water.

Amma felt something brush the bottom of one foot and then another as her legs moved involuntarily beneath her. Startled, she opened her eyes and twisted her waist to see if she had somehow ended up back near the shore. Apart from a thin line in the distance that she presumed was the way she had walked from, she saw only water in front of her.

Amma turned back in the opposite direction and then gave into the desire to scissor her legs back and forth beneath her. Again, her toes brushed something solid. Curious, instead of trying to back away she reached forward and attempted to pull herself through the water toward the thing, her intentions of self-destruction temporarily forgotten.

She couldn't be sure how far forward she had advanced before her arms smacked down onto something gritty several inches below the water. Amma tried to grip the coarse area, but her fingers couldn't find a good place to latch onto. She moved her legs up toward her stomach and thudded into the side of it with her knees.

Still reaching forward with her arms, Amma moved one leg down the side in slow motion, allowing her toes to find a natural crease. She then repeated the process with her other leg. Once she was satisfied with her chances, she pushed upward in an attempt to hoist herself onto the platform.

The exterior scratched painfully at her skin as it rubbed against her. Once the top half of her body pressed into the shelf, she rolled onto her back and pushed herself into a sitting position upon it. The mass hadn't moved at all under her weight, which led her to believe that it was a natural growth rooted to the ocean floor.

Amma doubted that the ocean would reject her a second time, and she reached forward, feeling for the edge on the other side and wondering if she should slide back off to continue with her plan. When her fingers reached what seemed to be the drop-off, she peered into the layer of cerulean blue water.

She could see a patchwork in shades of browns, pinks, and dull oranges. To her surprise, the structure didn't look as solid as it felt below her. Plants in alien shapes protruded from the top and in random intervals throughout it as far down the sides as she could see. Small holes, ridges, and cracks also seemed to line the exterior, and Amma watched as small creatures moved in and out of them all around her. Some moved on long, spindly legs and others swam. None of them seemed bothered by her presence.

Amma lifted her head to the sky. The more time she spent away from her dreary village, the less she understood why they weren't allowed to leave it. Confusion swirled within her. Of all the living creatures she had encountered since coming to the shore, none of them had gone out of their way to harm her. Even the ocean itself had refused to end her life.

She felt the pang of disappointment well up, and she understood that she had never really wanted to find answers. The truth was, from the moment she had dropped the bloodied rock in the sand, she had been seeking death, taunting it with her actions, but it had refused to accept her. Amma tugged at a strand of her hair, wrapping it around her finger as she thought, unsure of how she felt about the questions that were forming within her.

The only monsters she had ever met were back there, where she had come from, and Amma wondered if her great grandparents could have been lying all along to keep the others compliant. That would have made them the worst monsters of all. Amma gulped and winced as pain radiated from her throat and lungs.

She released her hair and reached for her neck, anticipating the familiar feel of her hand against it. She was startled by how rough her touch felt. Amma pulled her hand away to look at it, crinkling her nose at the sight. The skin on her palm looked weathered and rigid. As she inspected herself further, she found that her feet and toes were in a similar state. Distracted by the find, she barely registered the fact that the cold water began rippling beside her as something stirred in the distance.

When a sharp, slapping noise reached her ears, Amma looked up with a jerk. Several droplets of water rained down on her face and head from the apparent impact as she searched out the cause of the disturbance in the otherwise calm water.

Inky dark eyes watched her from only a short distance away, and as Amma's gaze locked onto them, the creature tilted her head up, exposing a very feminine-looking mouth and chin. A tight-lipped smile spread across its ashen blue lips, and Amma found herself smiling back.

The woman seemed to sink lower in the water and then began to propel herself in Amma's general direction, although she seemed to be moving sideways, as the crustacean had. By her trajectory, Amma guessed, the woman would pass by her from several feet away before she too would hit the hard, rock-like barrier. As the seconds ticked by, Amma bit her tongue lightly to keep herself from speaking, out of fear of scaring the stranger off.

When the woman reached the edge of the precipice, Amma watched in amazement as she pulled forward and hoisted herself up in one swift movement. The long, wet hair on her head hung limply around her impossibly oval face before cascading, unsnarled to her waist, covering her shoulders and chest in between.

Where her hair met her waistline, elegant fins protruded from her sides, the way the fanning leaves of a palm frond did. Just below that, where Amma would have expected legs to be, a sleek tail emerged. In the light, the scales shimmered in every color imaginable. Amma's breath caught in her throat at the sight, and much like when she first viewed the seashore, she found it hard to tear her eyes away.

As if the fish-woman enjoyed her inspection, she leaned forward and reached along the surface with her webbed fingers, stretching out and exposing another fin that protruded from her spine. When she righted herself again, the creature raised her hand and pointed one sharp black fingernail in her direction before motioning at her to come closer.

She began to inch across the surface but hesitated when the creature shifted position, opening her arms wide as if to embrace her and revealing dark veins that ran below the surface of her taut, translucent skin.

Amma opened her mouth to speak, but instead the sound of crashing waves filled her ears. The hair on the back of her neck prickled, and the world around her became hazy. Something cold touched her ankle, then encircled it, and Amma felt herself lurch forward as a sharp pain spread up her leg. She tried to call out as the pain crept farther up into her abdomen, but her brain seemed unable to accept her commands.

As the sharp, stabbing sensation reached her chest, the world she had been born into dissolved around her, replaced by strange images that seemed to flash into focus, then wink back out of existence before her very eyes. The images brought with them a feeling of euphoria that seemed to wrap around her entire body like a thick blanket.

Yareli Part Two ~ The Return

Yareli knew the strange dreams that played out in Amma's mind would leave her feeling confused when she woke. It was how the venom of her bite worked during the exchange. She would see Amma's memories, and the girl would see hers, only unlike the humans that she infected with her poison, she could be selective in what memories she shared.

A smile spread across the sleeping girl's face and Yareli supposed the human was dreaming that she was gliding through the water with ease. She would be feeling giddy and carefree as explosions filled the sky overhead with flashes of fire and light, which left strange colored auras on the horizon. The memory would fill her with a cheerfulness that she had never really experienced, although she wouldn't be quite sure why.

Usually, Yareli delighted in seeing the expressions on her victims' faces as she showed them the horrors that had befallen humankind over the decades. But unlike her past victims, something about the girl's memories had caused her to pity the human.

It had been the reason Yareli held back, deciding not to finish the girl off then and there. She had wanted to give her a chance to feel real joy once before her life ended.

Yareli had seen enough of the 747 passengers' memories to know their history well enough. Even without the strong toxins that were coursing through her veins, there was little chance of the girl deciphering the true meaning of the things she saw in her head. After all, in the time her great-grandparents had come from, the race of merpeople had still been believed to be nothing more than legend.

It would be another century before they first confronted the humans, pleading with them to stop destroying the planet. But even though disease had caused famine and the humans' numbers dwindled exponentially, they would not accept the species' wisdom. By all accounts, humans decided that merpeople were nothing more than amphibious creatures to be hunted down and experimented on.

This too was before Yareli's time. Another decade would pass before she would even be born. In her time, the merpeople had retreated back underwater to the deepest depths, where they had survived undetected for millennia.

Yareli leaned forward and twisted herself around in the coarse sand as she looked for a good spot to write 32,854 next to Amma's prone body.

She had dragged her back to the shore, where the shadow of the 747 would block much of the sun from reaching her exposed skin until she awakened. It wasn't far from the place where Yareli had watched her enter the ocean only hours before.

She closed her eyes and crinkled her nose. Her head throbbed when she tried to concentrate. It was always like that when someone else's memories were dancing around in her brain, at least until the transformation was over.

She peered out into the water and followed the lightly rolling waves with her eyes as they made their way onto the shore, stopping mere inches from where Amma's toes rested. Blood trickled down from her ankle to her heel before meeting the sand.

To better inspect the damage that she had inflicted with her bite, Yareli wiped at the blood with her webbed fingers, revealing the small but deep incisions. They formed a crude circle just above Amma's ankle.

Fresh blood began seeping from the bite again almost instantly, and Yareli furrowed her brow at the sight. She didn't want Amma incapacitated.

She used her arms to pull herself toward the shore in search of seaweed to cover the wound. Within minutes she found a nice clump that had gathered near the edge and worked to untangle it with her fingers. Once she separated a piece that looked both long and wide enough to dress the wound, she made her way back to the girl.

Yareli fastened the seaweed around her leg as tightly as possible. She could only hope that the makeshift bandage would hold up when Amma started to move about. There wasn't anything else she could do for the human. She was already starting to shed.

She reached out to pick up one of her discarded scales and looked it over. Yareli had almost forgotten how smooth the surface and edges felt between her fingers. A lot of time had passed for her since she had last taken a human form. It shimmered as the light caught it, revealing the familiar delicate netted pattern that covered the scale on both sides, and she was relieved.

Yareli had long wondered if the strange radiation that affected the island would one day cause changes to her own physiology. So far, it hadn't seemed to harm her or the other inhabitants, no matter the length of time they remained trapped here.

She shivered as a chill crept up her spine, and the hair on the back of her neck bristled. Yareli tensed and turned to face the girl, releasing the scale as she moved. It came as no surprise to her that the human was still sound asleep. The shore on this side of the island always awakened an unease within her.

Like many of the discarded items that littered the sand, it was the very place that she would find herself each time she tried to swim a good distance beyond the reef, as if picked up and transplanted by an unseen force.

Another chill ran through her. Yareli drew her mouth into a straight line and attempted to ignore the feeling. She needed to concentrate on her plan. She had never let anyone live very long after biting them before, and she would need to take some precautions if she wanted it to go smoothly.

Amma wasn't stupid. Yareli knew that she would eventually realize she had met the monster from her ancestors' stories and try to follow her. What she wasn't sure of was how long it would take before she started to make her way back to the village. She didn't like the idea of both of them showing up at the same time, identical to one another in almost every way.

Deciding it would be best to put a little distance between herself and the human as she transformed, Yareli moved down the shoreline. The changes took time, but when they were complete, she would be just as agile on the land as she was in water.

Once she had dragged herself several yards from the human, she scanned the area with fresh eyes. From there she could still see the clear outline of Amma's slumped form by the airplane. The stretch of beach between them appeared undisturbed, other than the grooves she had left as she moved with her tail still attached and a few scattered scales.

Yareli sat back in the wet part of the sand and allowed her tail to be cleaned by the gentle waves in order to avoid leaving an abundance of evidence in plain sight. She watched transfixed as each new surge washed away some of her scales, until only a sprinkling of them remained.

When her tail began to separate into two newly formed legs, the water stung at her splitting flesh. She couldn't hold back the pained hiss that escaped her throat as she pulled them back away from the salty water, midtransformation.

As Yareli waited for her new feet to finish forming, she stared hard in Amma's direction, looking for any sign of movement and rubbing her itchy hands together impatiently. The motion caused the now filmy skin on her palms and between her fingers to shred. She fought the urge to peel away the hanging flesh.

Once it was safe to stand, she moved toward the tree line. Her own nails were much too long and sharp for the job, and like her teeth, they wouldn't change with the rest of her. The process of ridding herself of the decaying flesh would be much quicker and a lot less messy if she used the bark from one of the trees to help loosen the old, dead skin.

She made her way toward the trenches, remembering that many of the trees in that spot had been damaged when the bomber came down. There, it wouldn't be hard to find one that she could tear a nice-sized piece of bark from.

After she sloughed the dead tissue from her hands, revealing the new, lightly tanned flesh beneath, she pulled the once translucent skin from her face and arms. When she was satisfied that her upper torso matched her newly formed lower half, she wadded the white and gray flesh into a ball and tossed it down into one of the trenches, then kicked fresh dirt toward the mess to help conceal it.

She gnashed her teeth as she caught a glimpse of the faded green cloth at the bottom, and the realization that she had forgotten to take Amma's clothes sunk in. Her choice to let the girl live, even if it was only temporary, was becoming more of a hassle than she had anticipated.

She clenched her fists in frustration and turned to the other trench. When she did, Amma's memory of discovering the site surfaced, as well as her recollection of the plane going down in her childhood.

As the scenes played out, Yareli was taken by Amma's curiosity and her desire to help. The urge to share her own recollections of the soldiers and how they had ended up on the island filled her, but she pushed the compulsion away. There would be time to share more memories with Amma later, after she disposed of the other villagers, if she still felt the urge to.

Yareli hopped into the trench, landing hard but gracefully on her new feet. She reached down and retrieved the ratty material, tearing it into two uneven strips of cloth in one effortless movement. She then tied the longer piece around her waist and used the second half to cover her exposed chest in a similar way before pulling herself up out of the hole with one arm.

Back at the top, Yareli's hands trembled with excitement as she peered into the wooded area in front of her, trying to get her bearings. She liked to think she knew the island pretty well, but it had been quite a while since she explored it.

Small details here changed rather quickly, and since Amma hadn't been allowed to leave the confines of the village often, Yareli couldn't rely solely on their combined knowledge as she moved forward.

She would have to take things slow until she found the markers Amma had learned to look for. It made sense that there wouldn't be any near the beach, given the humans' fear of the water that surrounded the island.

Armed with the understanding that the village was somewhere in the center, Yareli moved forward in a straight line, assuming the tactic would lead her in the right direction until she found one of the markers that would show her the path to get home.

Yareli focused her attention on the trees as she moved farther inland. Before long, she found one with two distinct vertical lines carved just above her eye level. Sure that this was what she had been looking for, she picked up her pace. A short way ahead, she found another marker. This one had two of the same vertical lines with a smaller horizontal line running through the bottom. She turned to her left and moved forward.

Continuing onward, she counted six more similar markers, some with the line through the bottom, indicating a left turn, and some with a line through the top, which indicated to go right. By the time she came across the seventh marker, her heart was racing with anticipation.-

She steadied herself against the tree and willed her heart to slow. Beyond the usual carvings for a right turn, a large X had been added below the image. To Amma, the letter used in this capacity signified a place where humans thought they shouldn't tread. Yareli turned to her left, furrowing her brow. She wanted to know why the warning was there.

She took a few slow cautious steps forward before reaching down to pick up a sturdy-looking limb that had broken off one of the trees. She gripped her weapon with such force that her knuckles ached.

Ahead of her, a spherical object protruded up from the forest floor, as if it had come down with such force, the ground had impacted, forming a crater beneath it. Broken branches, leaves, and other forest debris littered the area. Light streamed down from the sky where an opening in the canopy had been made as the thing crashed through.

Beads of sweat formed on her forehead as she looked at the aircraft from beyond her own time. She stepped into the light and reached her empty hand out to touch the surface. It felt warm from the sun's rays. She wiped away some of the crusty debris, clearing a small area and revealing the interior of the object.

Although the image inside still appeared distorted, Yareli could make out the empty seat that was mounted at the center, and even though she knew the pilot had not returned to his ship since it landed, she bit at her lip and leaned against the sphere to try to see more.

After she had become trapped here, he had been the first of many humans to arrive, from many different places, but he had been the only one that had ever come from a time further in history than Yareli's own.

This time it was her own memory that invaded her senses. She had gone to the surface near one of the few remaining occupied cities because she had been curious and willful. She hadn't held such hatred for the humans back then. She had never met one, and to her, the stories about them were just that. They didn't feel real. Yareli had wanted to see them for herself, despite the warnings of her elders.

As Yareli rose up toward the surface, she could hear muffled shouting and feel the vibrations of explosions nearby. Regardless of that, the idea of being in the midst of an ongoing war didn't deter her.

Instead, she moved closer to the shore and popped her head above the surface. The noise amplified and seemed to surround her. The change had been so sudden that she became disoriented. She didn't fight back as she felt herself getting pulled onto the shore by the current.

Lying flat on her back with her body half in and out of the water, Yareli listened to the sounds that echoed all around her, trying to differentiate one from another. But the blasts and shouts seemed to meld in a horrifying chorus.

She flipped herself over and sat up, focusing on the cityscape in the distance. As she did, the combination of the chemicals and ash in the air made her eyes sting, causing her to squint. The buildings were shrouded in hazy smoke. Yareli could see only a vague outline of the strange machines that roamed the man-made streets below them and the darkening sky above.

A moan nearby caught her attention, and she scanned the shore for the first time. Slain soldiers seemed to lie in every direction. They all wore uniforms of either pale green or a combination of dark grays and blues. Bugs swarmed above the corpses of both factions as their blood soaked into the ground.

Yareli wondered how much time had passed since the fighting had moved on from this spot. The sight filled her with disgust, and yet she lingered. Her curiosity only grew deeper the longer she stayed. Another moan, this one feebler than the first, sounded close by, and she turned her head in search of the survivor.

She caught sight of the soldier just as he managed to pull himself up to his knees. The man's hair and skin were so fair that even in the dimming light she could see the blood that seeped from a gash on his scalp, trickling down one side of his face.

As their eyes locked, Yareli's heart thumped. Instinct warned her to flee. Wounded animals were dangerous and unpredictable, after all. But she was enthralled with the idea of finally meeting a living, breathing human.

The soldier grunted as he pushed himself forward into a crawling position, and Yareli watched, unfazed, as he began to move his lean body in her direction. She grinned as he got within arm's length and sat back on his knees once again.

He reached forward with one hand and latched onto her hair. Stunned, Yareli didn't react until he raised his other hand in her direction, aiming a long, serrated knife at her chest.

She furrowed her brow as she reached up to block the weapon. The soldier's grip was so loose on the knife that the force made it fall from his hand. Angry, Yareli shoved the man backward, causing him to collapse, sprawled out in the dirt.

His eyes darted around in delirium as she leaned over him. She doubted that he had ever recognized her for what she was. Her anger dissipated, and for a moment she considered biting him to see his memories, but she had no desire to take his form and walk about on human legs.

Instead, she left him as he was and turned back to the water. Night had fallen, and Yareli knew it wouldn't be long before the scavengers would appear and descend on the bodies.

She had stayed close to the surface as she began to swim away, when a loud, cracking noise exploded above her, causing her to spin back in the direction she had come from. This blast was different than the ones she had heard earlier.

In the distance, a column of smoke rose from the city. It spread out farther the higher it got, until she could no longer make out the silvery moon hanging against the backdrop of stars that normally blanketed the sky.

Yareli looked away. She didn't need to see more to understand why her race steered clear of the humans. Relief washed over her as more smaller explosions followed, relighting the sky above her in sudden bursts.

Perhaps this was the end her people had been waiting for. Embracing the idea of returning to her home to share what she had seen and giddy at the prospect that her theory was correct, she eagerly resumed her course.

Sometime later, as Yareli was passing a small group of islands, solid gray masses began to rain down from the sky, leaving trails of smoke behind them. This alone wouldn't have frightened her, but as she looked on, she noticed that the water didn't splash up when the falling objects made contact. Instead, it sizzled and bubbled as they broke the outer surface before beginning to descend.

Rather than diving deeper, in an attempt to avoid contact with them Yareli decided to seek shelter. The islands in the area were known to have many hidden underwater caves that were sometimes used by merpeople as they traveled far distances because they were especially hard for humans to access.

She moved toward the closest island and entered the first opening she came to that was well below the surface. The arched entranceway was almost too small for Yareli, but she squeezed in and pulled herself along the walls until she came to a larger grotto where she could turn around.

Below her, there seemed to be another much bigger opening that led out of the cave. The light that made its way through was a brilliant blue. To her surprise and amusement, she found that anywhere this light touched, her unsubmerged frame appeared to glow in response, and she turned in a circle, looking for a way to get out of the water.

There was only one place were a rocky shelf protruded from the wall. The ledge was long and narrow but seemed wide enough for her to sit upon without too much discomfort, and although it was too high above her to be able to see onto it, she was confident that her strong arms could hoist her up.

She moved toward it and lifted one of her webbed hands over her head to clamp her fingers around the edge. Testing her weight against it, she pulled downward with all her strength to see if the rock would crumble in her grasp.

When it didn't, she lifted her other hand, and as she reached forward, something solid beyond her view grazed her fingers then shifted away as she gripped the ledge to begin pulling her body upward. Just when the view on top came into focus, she caught a glimpse of the object's ovular form roll off the edge.

If not for the sight in front of her, she would have followed its descent with her eyes, but they had landed on what seemed to her like thousands of small bone fragments that spanned the length of the shelf. They appeared to have been there a while, completely devoid of muscle, flesh, or scales.

A soft splash sounded as the falling object came into contact with the surface of the water below, and Yareli reached out to pick up one of the remaining pieces, her original intentions for reaching the shelf forgotten.

She doubted that the bones had been carried inside by the ocean water.

The delicate fragments were very similar in color, and they didn't seem to be scattered across the rocks haphazardly but rather formed a long, slender triangle, as if they were the rough outline of some creature's shape.

Yareli returned the shard to its resting place and looked toward what she thought would have been the upper torso, wondering what was missing. If it had been an oval-shaped skull that she had knocked loose, the creature would have looked very humanoid in origin, but the bones seemed too thin and pliable to be from a land dweller. The grisly image her thoughts inspired caused her to release her hold.

As she slipped back down, the effect of the water rippling around with her movement caused eerie mermaid-shaped shadows to sway against the cavern walls. A knot formed in her abdomen as she watched them move back and forth, coming close together but never quite meeting in the middle.

Unsettled and ashamed that she might have disturbed the final resting place of one of her own people, she closed her eyes as she turned away. Eager to put distance between herself and the bones, she headed back the way she had come, moving as quickly as the tight passage would allow.

She stopped just inside the small opening. Once there, she remained at the entrance, watching to see if any of the chunky objects would hit the surface and sink down in front of her. When none did, after several minutes she grew impatient and left the cover of the cave.

When she resurfaced to be sure it was over, the feeling of unease that the bones had caused her finally lifted, and she was filled with relief at the sight of the clear sky and the sun that shone brightly overhead. It wasn't until she attempted to resume her journey home that Yareli realized she was trapped.

Yareli closed her eyes and sighed, pitying herself as the memory of her arrival on the island continued to play out.

Since Yareli had spent most of her life in the deepest depth of the ocean, several days passed before she had taken notice of the sun and the fact that it no longer disappeared from the sky at times when only the moon should have been present.

That was precisely what she had been sitting near the shore, thinking about when she caught sight of the round craft in the sky. It had appeared within the blue space between the sun and moon out of nowhere. As the vessel moved forward in an angled trajectory, speeding toward the island, Yareli had hoped it carried help; instead it had carried a uniformed soldier. The very same one that she had encountered on the shore before she began her journey home. Caught off guard by the prospect, she distanced herself from the pilot and observed him from afar.

When she finally worked up the courage to confront him, she saw bloodlust in his eyes and mistook it for recognition. This time, she wasn't surprised when he lunged at her with his knife, and even though he was in much better health, she had still taken him down rather easily.

Yareli gave her head a shake as if it would rid her of the memories before she pushed herself upright. She managed to step backward just in time to see one of the familiar creeping red vines feeling its way toward her. She cursed herself under her breath, knowing she should have looked for the dangerous plant before stepping out into the light.

A few more moments pressed against the sphere and the vine would have been wrapped securely around her calf.

She thought of Amma and wondered if her curiosity would pull her away from her path as well. With nothing to cut it off, she would find herself in real danger. Once the vines had a grip on you, they would never let go. In fact, the more you struggled against them, the tighter they would squeeze.

Yareli reached down and grabbed the wriggling end of the vine. Even in their form she was much stronger than any human she had ever encountered. She lifted her foot and brought it down hard on the vine where it protruded from the ground, pulling it tight to hold it still. Then she took her nails and easily sliced through the creeping plant with her free hand. A thick pink liquid oozed from the severed sections as they landed on the ground, and as the remaining chunk she held went limp, she released it.

The piece still connected to the root retracted beneath the dirt. It was still alive, but it would be a long time before it was healed enough to attack again.

Yareli let out a low sigh and then spun on her heals and headed back to the last marker. She threw a fleeting glance toward the image carved into the tree again and then turned right, toward the village.

When Yareli took her first step onto the bridge, the only evident noise was the gurgling of the water below her and the steady thumping of her heart. She knew from Amma's memories that the humans had started to grow complacent. Still, at the very least she had expected to find someone up keeping watch as the others slept.

She moved on, making her way toward the fire pit closest to her. Long gray tendrils of smoke rose up from its center, but only a few hot embers remained glowing at its core. This would be easier than she thought.

She slipped into the first hovel and leaned down over the sleeping human. There was no need to bite the man. She doubted his memory harbored any useful information, and he was alone, so there would be no need to incapacitate him with her poison.

Instead, she lifted her hands to his face and neck, using one to effectively cover his mouth and nose while she positioned the sharp nails on her other hand at his throat, preparing to slice into the tender flesh on his neck, the same way she had slashed through the vine.

He jerked as his intake of air was interrupted, and when his eyes flung open in shock, she made a sweeping motion with her razor-sharp nails, severing everything in their path. A spray of blood shot from a perforated artery, and Yareli pressed her palm into his face harder as he tried to wiggle out of her grasp.

When the human stopped struggling, Yareli removed her hand and backed away. She would need a moment to compose herself before moving on. Violent interactions often opened a fissure, causing other memories to flood her mind, and this day was no exception.

Although she had learned about it as a youth, tasting a human's blood had been a new experience for Yareli. The soldier-turned-pilot's memories had been the first she had seen, and like a first kiss, the experience would never be forgotten.

When the memories arrived, she didn't understand why she found no recollection of herself and the night they had met on the battle-worn shore. For a moment she entertained the possibility that she had been mistaken about his identity, but as more of his memories surfaced, she noticed other inconsistencies. The past as she remembered it appeared to be wrong, not just regarding the humans, but her own kind as well.

Confused by the information, she did her best to construct a timeline and analyze what she saw. It seemed that this soldier had never joined the battlefront in that capacity, because that war had never happened. Instead, the race of man had set aside their differences and banded together in order to focus on a different threat: an impending mermaid invasion.

To Yareli's horror, the memories didn't stop there. She had given herself a front-row seat to several battles between the species, where to her it felt like she was slaughtering her own people.

Believing that she had been displaced, somehow removed from the world she knew and transplanted in an altered timeline where merpeople had been effectively wiped off the planet, helped her endure at first. But as more vessels started appearing, and she tested the memories of the humans, she realized her situation was more complex than that.

It wasn't she that had been displaced, but rather the entire island seemed to be affected. No matter what decade they came from, each new set of humans brought a version of history with slight differences that to her seemed even more devastating than the last. The ever-evolving destruction she saw at the hands of the humans haunted her, propelling her forward, giving her a purpose.

Yareli continued to move through the hovels as if on autopilot, slaying each human she found in quick succession, until all that remained were herself and Amma's attacker. With him she hesitated, wondering if Amma would have been relieved or disappointed that she hadn't killed him with the rock.

She reached down toward his sleeping form and gripped his exposed throat. When his eyes sprang open, she lifted him into the air, causing her nails to burrow deeper into his flesh. Hot, tacky blood leaked out onto her fingers and began running down her outstretched arm as she waited for him to see Amma in her before she squeezed. As she did, a euphoric feeling engulfed her, and she couldn't wait to show Amma what had become of him.

When Amma appeared in the doorway of her hovel with her shoulders slumped and her head down as she crossed the threshold, looking as if the sheer silence of her surroundings was weighing on her, Yareli was filled with disappointment.

She felt like she had grown closer to the girl through her memories than any of the humans she had bitten before. As she had waited, she had even toyed with the idea of keeping her around as a companion instead of finishing her off as planned.

It wasn't until her eyes met Yareli's that she stumbled backward, losing her footing in the process and landing with a thud on her backside. Her teeth knocked together with such force when she landed that Yareli imagined intense pain had to be radiating through her jaw and wondered if it been the reality of what she had caused crashing over her, or simply the fact that she wasn't alone that had thrown her off balance.

Surely seeing a reflection of oneself where there shouldn't be one could have a dizzying effect. The mermaid smiled wide, revealing a mouth filled with sharp, pointed teeth. Those teeth were the only notable difference between Amma and her doppelgänger, apart from the blood that smeared Yareli's body.

She could see Amma's throat constrict just before she let out a strangled scream. As if answering her cry, Yareli moved beside her. She had made a decision.

She drew her mouth into a straight line and licked at her lips. She could taste the sweetness of the dark liquid that beaded and dripped down into her mouth from her pointed canines. It had a sweet taste that lingered on her tongue, making it tingle.

She leaned down and sank her teeth into Amma's soft flesh. The only movement from Amma was the twitching of her muscles as the stinging heat of the venom was reintroduced into her bloodstream. When she was sure Amma's senses were dulled and the haze had fallen back around her, she retracted.

The first time Yareli had done it, she had only meant to share events that had brought her joy and would help comfort her victim. This time she wouldn't just show Amma a few memories. She would show her all of them, and not just her own but also the memories of every single human she had bitten, starting from the beginning. She would know the truth of the situation, and then she could decide if she wanted to live forever stuck in this trap with her or die.

Alternate Version of Events ~ The Return (Amma)

A strange dream played out in her mind, and to Amma it was as if she was the fish creature. She glided through the water with ease, feeling giddy and carefree as explosions filled the sky overhead with flashes of fire and light that left strange colored auras on the horizon. Something exciting was happening to the world. The human race had managed to bring itself to extinction.

Amma sat up with a start and twisted herself around in the coarse sand. A hint of the bizarre dream remained, and although she wasn't sure why, she was filled with a cheerfulness that she rarely experienced.

She thought perhaps the dream lifted her spirits because in it the humans didn't seem to behave any better than the survivors that were stuck on the island with her.

Amma chewed at her bottom lip, wishing she had someone to share her recent experiences with. Someone that could help her make sense of the things she had encountered.

It dawned on her that she was back on the shore of the island, not far from the spot where she remembered entering the water. The shadow of the 747 blocked much of the sun from her view.

The numbers 32,854 were written in the sand next to her. Amma closed her eyes and crinkled her nose as she thought back. She didn't recall making the impression, but her head and her ankle both throbbed as she tried to concentrate.

"Mermaid" she whispered, cocking her head to the side. Amma couldn't remember hearing it before, and yet it was somehow familiar. With its use, her mind conjured up a fuzzy image of the fish woman, as if it was a distant memory.

Had the creature returned her to the shore? She smiled. The very thought of the mermaid brought her a feeling of peace.

Amma jerked her head around, looking for the mysterious creature, but there was no one to be seen. She peered out into the water and followed the lightly rolling waves with her eyes as they made their way onto the shore, stopping mere inches from where her toes rested. Blood trickled down from her ankle to her heel before meeting the sand.

Amma pushed herself to her feet and took a few steps forward. At first, the water tickled at her toes as it swirled around them, but when the cool liquid met the wound, the throbbing pain was replaced by a sharp stinging. She hurried to wash the blood away before stepping back out of the water in order to better inspect the damage.

Fresh blood was already seeping from the wound again, and Amma furrowed her brow at the sight. She had expected to find a long scrape or a jagged cut from her time in the water. Instead she found small but deep incisions that formed a crude circle just above her ankle.

She reached for a clump of the seaweed that had gathered near the shore and worked to untangle it with her fingers. Once she separated a piece that looked both long enough to tie around her leg and wide enough to cover her wound, Amma fastened it around her ankle as tightly as she could.

After she righted herself, she scanned the beach with fresh eyes. This time she spotted a trail of footprints that started in the wet part of the sand a little farther down the shore. As she got closer, she couldn't help but notice with each new gentle rolling wave, a fresh sprinkling of shiny ovular scales was added to the shore's edge.

Out of curiosity, Amma reached down and grasped one. It shimmered as the light caught it, and although she could see that a delicate netted pattern covered the scale on both sides, its surface and edges felt smooth between her fingers.

She drew her mouth into a straight line and chewed at her lip thoughtfully. Upon further inspection, she found that the scale was too hard to bend or tear with her fingers.

Amma shivered as a chill crept up her spine and the hair on the back of her neck bristled. She tensed and spun around, releasing the scale as she moved.

Again, she searched the beach with her eyes, but she didn't see any movement in the distance. Instead, as she scanned the shoreline in her immediate view, she was reminded of the mermaid. With the memory, the nagging feeling of unease that had boiled up within her depleted, and Amma refocused her attention back to her original objective: the footprints.

They didn't look fresh to her. If they were, the ones closest to the shore would have been filled at least partially with seawater. She placed a foot beside one of the imprints then shifted her weight to press down into the damp sand. When she lifted it, her stomach fluttered.

The impressions leading out of the water were very similar in appearance to the one she had just made. If Amma hadn't known better, she would have thought they were her own footprints, but they didn't lead anywhere near the spot she had awakened in.

She followed the impressions until they disappeared in the dryer sand. When Amma looked around herself, she found that she was just about halfway from the shore to the tree line. Careful to mimic the steps behind her, she continued forward to see where whomever left the footprints would have ended up if they had moved along the same path.

She paused as she reached the trenches and peered down into one, then the other. The first hole held the same faded green cloth she had seen before, but the second trench had become a depository for what looked to her like shredded flesh.

For the most part, the discarded skin had a translucent appearance, although there were several noticeable white and gray patches. Amma released an uncontrolled gasp as she backed away from the hole and allowed herself to sink to her knees.

She was missing something. She knew it. Even though the throbbing had subsided in her ankle and head, she still found it hard to concentrate. It felt as if she had been trying to work herself out from behind a curtain from the moment she had awakened.

Amma clenched her fists in frustration. An idea was there that was just out of reach.

She took a deep breath and unclenched her hands, revealing the slight indents her nails had made in her palms, and she wondered if a good dose of pain could bring her back to reality.

She took a deep breath and exhaled, readying herself. Then she closed her eyes and opened her jaw as wide as it would go as she lifted her wrist to her mouth. Once in position, she snapped her jaw shut, forcing her teeth into the flesh on her arm until her mouth was filled with the iron taste of her own blood and something unfamiliar. A sweet taste that lingered on her tongue, making it tingle.

She opened her eyes and studied her new wound. The indentations of her teeth were clearly defined, even in the places where she hadn't broken the skin, yet she had barely felt it. Her cheeks flushed.

She lowered her arm and pulled her legs out from beneath herself. When she tore the seaweed from her wound, she was relieved to see that the wound had now crusted over and was no longer seeping blood.

Amma held her wounded arm close to her damaged leg and compared the marks. The impressions on her arm were not deep, like the ones on her ankle, but she couldn't deny that the size and shape of the outlines held similarities. Had the mermaid bitten her?

Just as the thought occurred, the world tilted beneath her, and she lashed out to stop herself from falling forward. Amma giggled as her outstretched hands hit the ground in front of her. She turned sideways and lowered herself the rest of the way down until she was lying with her cheek in the dirt, staring straight ahead.

Images of large machines and people she couldn't quite focus on filled her vision. A feeling of hope blossomed inside her as the humans in crisp white clothes vanished, replaced by haggard, bloodied versions of themselves. Then the sky exploded in the same colorful display she remembered from her dream. This time, as the excitement filled her, so did a nagging urge to return to her people.

When the images stopped, Amma stood. Her legs trembled as she peered into the wooded area in front of her, trying to get her bearings. She needed to go home. The desire overwhelmed her senses.

Amma tried her best to move forward in a straight line from her position by the trenches. Since the village was at the center of the island, she hoped that the tactic would aid her in finding her way back.

Her task was made more difficult by bouts of dizziness that seemed to assault her out of nowhere as she was walking along, causing her to stop. When she did, the desire to move would build up inside her, and her heart would begin to race.

It felt like she had been moving in this way for half of the day when during one of her dizzy spells she steadied herself against a tree with two distinct vertical lines carved just above her eye level. Even in her frenzied state she recognized the markings. It was one of the discreet ways the first generation of survivors had kept track of their trails.

Amma focused her attention on the trees and picked up her pace. A short way ahead, she found another marker. This one had two of the same vertical lines, with a smaller horizontal line running through the bottom. She turned to her left and moved ahead.

Continuing on, she counted six more similar markers, some with the line through the bottom, indicating a left turn, and some with a line through the top, which indicated to go right. By the time she came across the seventh marker, her dizzy spells had ceased, and although the urgent desire for her to return to her people remained, it no longer pulled at her with the same fierceness.

Amma was relieved by the change, because this marker perplexed her. Beyond the usual carvings for a right turn, a large X had been added below the image. She turned to her left, furrowing her brow. She had never heard of an X being used on the trails, and she wanted to know why it was there.

Amma felt beads of sweat form on her forehead as she took a few slow, cautious steps forward, before reaching down to pick up a sturdy-looking limb that had broken off one of the trees. She gripped her weapon with such force that her knuckles ached.

Ahead of her, a spherical object protruded up from the forest floor, as if it had come down with such force, the ground had impacted, forming a crater beneath it. Broken branches, leaves, and other forest debris littered the area. Light streamed down from the sky, where an opening in the canopy had been made as the thing crashed through it.

She stepped into the light and reached her empty hand out to touch the surface. It felt warm from the sun's rays. She wiped at some of the debris with her hand, clearing away a small area and revealing the interior of the object. An empty seat was mounted inside at the center. Amma leaned against the sphere to try to see more, but like the plane at the beach, the image was distorted by the filth that covered the sphere.

She pushed herself upright and stepped backward just in time to see one of the familiar creeping red vines feeling its way toward her. She cursed herself under her breath, knowing she should have looked for the dangerous plant before stepping out into the light.

A few more moments pressed against the sphere and the vine would have been wrapped securely around her calf. With nothing to cut it off, she would have been in real danger. Once the vines had a grip on you, they would never let go. In fact, the more you struggled against them, the tighter they would squeeze.

She sighed and headed back toward the last marker, thinking of her mother and the venomous bite she had sustained from the lizard. For a moment she wondered if the same fate had befallen her. But as the thought entered her mind, it was wiped away by the memory of the mermaid. With it, Amma's worry seemed to melt as the curtain of haze settled back into place.

She threw a fleeting glance toward the image carved into the tree again and then turned right, toward the village.

When Amma took her first step onto the bridge, the only noise that was evident was the gurgling of the water below her and the steady thumping of her heart. At the very least, she had expected to find someone up, keeping watch as the others slept.

She moved forward, making her way toward the fire pit closest to her. Long gray tendrils of smoke rose up from its center, but only a few hot embers remained glowing at its core. She crossed her arms over her chest and rubbed at the goosebumps that had formed there as she turned to move in the direction of her own hovel.

As she walked through the village, the euphoric feeling that had engulfed her, pushing her forward, dissipated once again and her shoulders slumped, as if the sheer silence weighed them down. Something was not right, but she couldn't stop. She needed to get home.

When Amma reached the doorway and crossed the threshold, revealing the interior, the reality of what she had done crashed over her with such suddenness that she stumbled backward, losing her footing in the process. She landed with a thud on her backside, causing her teeth to knock together with such force that pain radiated through her jaw. She wasn't alone.

The creature that stood across the room, staring back at her, held such a strong resemblance to Amma that it seemed as if she was looking into the clear ocean water again, viewing her own reflection.

The mermaid smiled wide, exposing a mouth filled with sharp, pointed teeth. Those teeth were the only notable difference between Amma and her doppelgänger, apart from the blood that smeared the creature's chin.

Amma's throat constricted, and she let out a strangled cry as she recalled the sense of danger she had felt on the beach after finding the scales and the discarded skin. Anger at herself welled up within her, because somewhere deep down she had known from the moment she had awakened by the 747, and yet she had pushed her own intuition away with such careless ease.

As if answering her cry, in what seemed like one effortless movement, the mermaid was at her side. To Amma, she appeared to be just as agile on land as she did among the waves.

The creature now hovered over her, smiling gaily.

From this proximity, Amma could see that several of her pointed teeth were longer than the others. On the tips of these canines, a dark liquid beaded and dripped down into the mermaid's mouth.

Amma understood that this toxic substance and its residual effects had been the reason she was unable to acknowledge the truth of their meeting for what it was. It had subdued her, making her feel calm and euphoric as it wore on in her system. Then when she had bitten herself, taking it back in through her mouth, it had altered the effects somewhat.

Amma gulped and closed her eyes, resigned to her fate.

She felt the mermaid lean in closer, and she winced as the teeth sank into her flesh.This time, Amma swore she could feel the stinging heat of the venom as it mixed with her blood. When the haze once again began to fall down around Amma and her senses dulled, she felt the mermaid retract, showing restraint.

In some far corner of her mind she wondered why the mermaid would want to slow the process. Amma focused all of her remaining faculties on opening her eyes.

When she finally managed the feat, the mermaid lifted her face to Amma and gazed into them for several seconds before Amma's vision blurred.

The pictures once again played out, albeit the loop seemed to be moving much slower this time. As the images paraded by, she found that with them came strong emotions and knowledge of things that she had never seen or heard of.

She witnessed people fighting in crowded places and recognized it as war. She saw the men in white coats and understood that they were scientists like her great-grandparents had been. Then the strange machines appeared, and as the explosions filled the sky, Amma felt both comfort and exhilaration at the idea that the human race destroyed itself.

Instead of being horrified, Amma giggled and fidgeted. She wasn't in control of her feelings, but she was still together enough to understand that the things she saw were memories the mermaid chose to share with her.

The first time the creature had done it, she had only shared events that brought her joy in order to keep her victim docile until she was unconscious, allowing the mermaid to root through her memories and find the others.

An urgent desire to go home bloomed within Amma, and she felt like she was beneath the waves, swimming once more. A sentry for her people, she needed to report back to them that they were finally free of the human menace. Only as she had moved passed the nearby islands, something unseen had pulled her inland.

After that, every time she moved a good distance beyond the reef, she was pushed back to this island's shore. When the memories danced forward, she felt the mermaid's apprehension as she watched the sky and realized time no longer played by the same rules here.

Then the feeling was quickly swept away, replaced by another.

The horror gripped her when she finally understood the full truth of the place.

She was stuck in a trap, a human experiment gone wrong, and she would never get out. Her hatred for the race grew with each new human arrival, no matter what time they came from, and she took pleasure in wiping them back out.

The understanding must have shown in Amma's eyes, because at that moment the mermaid lowered her face and bit down again.

A scream reverberated inside Amma's head as the spittle ran down her chin.

About the Author

M. Ainihi is a passionate dark fantasy author, proud mother, wife, and adventurer. Hailing from the wilds of Upstate New York and Currently residing in the Chicagoland area, The Warning Signs is her first completed short story collection.

Also by M. Ainihi

Rise: A Blood Inheritance Novel

Most humans do not know about the existence of the outer realms, or the fierce battles that once waged between the magical races before thier creation. But for teen Amanda, ever since she encountered the jinni in the forest, it's her new reality, a lace where darkness lies around every corner, and she's lost almost all hope of surviving it.

Lost: A Blood Inheritance Novel

Before Amanda knew about the seven realms, she longed to know her mother. Now her inherited gift is the very thing she fears most, and even as she fights to keep the shadow magic at bay, she can feel it growing inside her. Plagued by nightmares and haunted by a new vision of Emily, a cryptic accusation may just send her tumbling over the edge.

Endow: A Blood Inheritance Novel

Endow takes Amanda, Emily, and Kiami on a dangerous trip through the realms. Amanda is determined to prove that the stones they were given are the very ones from the ancient myth. To do so she may have to divulge a few of her dark secrets.

Resist: A Blood Inheritance Novel

Coming soon...